Bushranger's Mountain

Victoria Gordon

Harlequin Books

TORONTO • NEW YORK • LONDON
AMSTERDAM • PARIS • SYDNEY • HAMBURG
STOCKHOLM • ATHENS • TOKYO • MILAN

Original hardcover edition published in 1985
by Mills & Boon Limited

ISBN 0-373-02714-1

Harlequin Romance first edition September 1985

CHAPTER ONE

THE erratic, unmelodic yodelling of a hunting hound brought Leith abruptly awake, yanking her from a languid daydream to a reality that was scarcely more believable.

Shaking her white-blonde hair, she straightened in the lawn chair and glanced to her right, following the sound back to its hidden source on the bush-covered mountain.

Her mountain, she thought, a slow smile playing across her soft lips. Even after a week it seemed unreal, a bubble-dream so tenuous that she sometimes felt it must burst even as she watched.

Her eyes strayed fondly across the small dam where three ducks cruised, past the wattle tree she knew marked a permanent, flowing spring, over acres of green paddocks sprinkled with clumps of yellow daffodils, the spiky tufts of reeds, the darker green of the bracken ferns. Beyond the paddocks, the bush closed in again, rising up the steep slash where the power line descended, rising up then through scrub and timber until finally it began to thin out, giving way to the rocky summit that loomed above.

Her mountain ... not really hers, of course, but the presence of the rugged grey peak was so vital to her dream that she couldn't look at the mountain without a surge of prideful possessiveness.

The hound bellowed again, voice echoing down to swirl through the branches of the enormous pine trees that dominated the area Leith mentally termed the house paddock.

She looked up again at the sound, frowning slightly. Somebody was, she presumed, hunting wallabies up there, though she'd heard no shots ... only the banshee crying of the hound.

Pensively, she stared straight ahead then, her eyes drawn by the hazy blue of the hills far to the east. The colour was nebulous really, receding from the bright green of the tea-tree scrub closest to her, diminishing in brightness as the view stretched past the wattles on the crest of the ridge, across out-of-sight hillside paddocks to the next ridge, dark green with scrub, and finally to the hazy hills beyond Tea Tree and Brighton.

In the immediate foreground was the barn, an ancient red-and-grey structure that looked as if a puff of wind would send it spinning away. And yet, it was perhaps a century old, Leith knew, and constructed on a framework of foot-thick poles, the outer covering a series of hand-hewn slabs of native timber.

Around her, the riotous garden of native and imported shrubbery, now so overgrown, so untended despite her best intentions that it was almost more wilderness than garden.

And ... all hers! Thirty-nine point six seven hectares—so near a hundred acres the difference was negligible. Hers! It had been hers for a week, a full seven days, and yet she still found it quite impossible to believe.

Slouching back in the lawn chair, she prowled the range of her vision through eyes like pale grey velvet, surveying her property with an air so proprietorial she had to giggle at the realisation. Leith Larsen, property owner!

It *was* unbelievable. Scarcely a month ago she'd been a full-time secretary, part-time potter in Sydney. Now she was a land-owner, a full-time potter—or would be soon—with her very own property halfway up a mountain in Tasmania.

Leith closed her wide grey eyes and returned to her daydreaming, mind happily engrossed as it had been for a week in the planning of the rest of her dream. She could do it; she knew she could, now that the hardest part was accomplished. She would have to do it—her entire future was invested, along with the entire second-division lottery prize which had made it all possible.

Was that the price of a dream, she wondered, a weekly one-dollar lottery ticket come good? Smiling to herself, she added up the weekly dollars to reckon her dream property had cost her all of $11—a 5,000-to-1 lucky streak that could only be the beginning of an even brighter future.

Now she could work at her craft full-time, not in hours stolen from those in which she should have been resting, from weekends she could have spent on dates, on adventures. And surely, given such an opportunity, she could easily broaden her reputation as a potter with promise, a growing talent with artistic worlds to conquer.

She had her property, room to be self-sufficient, grow her own vegetables, raise her own food, a situation in which her savings could be stretched until her craft began to fully pay its own way.

She hadn't a debt in the world, and even optimistically her savings should provide a year in which to make the pottery pay, now that she'd paid the myriad charges of rates and telephone and electricity and legal fees and the hundred-and-one others that had cropped up during the property settlement.

A year! It would be enough. It must be. Even working part-time, she'd earned enough from her pottery . . . and now, with no rent to pay, none of the city expenses . . . well, she'd manage, anyway.

Her few friends, of course, thought she was utterly mad! Her announcement that she was abandoning the bright lights of Sydney had provoked howls of astonishment, even derision. And when she'd said she was not only going to Tasmania, but to someplace in the country, even her closest friends had shaken their heads in wonderment.

'But you're a city person. You'll go mad there,' one had said. 'Really, Leith, be sensible. And what about Brian?'

Brian! Even thinking of the name brought a shiver to Leith's pensive mood. Brian, the arch-sophisticate, had professed even more astonishment than anyone, but

Leith knew better—now—than to accept his attitude at face value.

Brian! Handsome, always perfectly groomed, always perfectly correct in his attention to detail, always charming, attentive, loving. And lying!

Even when she'd angrily confronted him with the evidence of his perfidy, he'd blatantly attempted to lie his way out of it, doing so with the smoothness of long practice, so obviously assured that Leith had always believed him in the past and would therefore continue to be easily deceived.

And when that ploy had failed, he'd switched tactics smoothly, using emotional blackmail as callously as he'd always used his immense charm.

'Oh, really, Leith. You're not running off to the wilds of Tasmania just because of this?' he'd scorned, blithely waving aside his indiscretions as being of no significance. Which they probably weren't—to him, Leith thought. But to her the open betrayal had been heart-wrenching despite the implied professional compliment involved.

At least, she thought, he hadn't bothered to try and deny the charge, though he equally didn't *admit* that he'd been keeping company with Leith only to assure his gallery a steady supply of her work. But he had done just that, spicing the relationship with just enough hints and promises of something much more lasting, especially when he was trying to set aside her inhibitions about extramarital sex.

And, at the end, trying so desperately to make her feel guilty, to shift the entire emphasis on to her slender shoulders, to use her own innocence as a weapon against her ... Leith shivered more strongly as her revulsion grew.

Well, it was over now ... and for the best, no question of that. And now, in retrospect, she couldn't even see her year with Brian as a waste. The emotional involvement, so ego-destroying there at the end, had been a marvellous tonic for her creative muse while it had lasted. And if nothing else, she now felt herself less gullible, less likely to be deceived in the future.

Not, Leith thought with a wry grin, that she expected her future to be filled with opportunistic scoundrels of Brian's type, nor any other type for that matter. No, she was on her own now, and so she'd stay, invulnerable in her independence and jealous of her right to lead her own life in her own way.

She might even take a leaf from Brian's book, she thought, then dismissed the idea as quickly as it came. She just wasn't the type to take undue advantage, and Leith knew herself well enough to realise she wasn't likely to change that aspect of her character. Not at the ripe old age of twenty-six and not in the midst of creating for herself the life-style she'd always dreamed of.

She made a mental note to remember this resolution. Especially, she thought, where it concerned Christopher Hardy, the young realtor who had astonished both of them by the ease with which he'd answered Leith's first tentative inquiry about where she might find the property she wanted.

'There's a place I saw when I was here on holiday two years ago,' she began, then went on to explain in great detail the dream property that had so caught her fancy she could still recall every detail.

The young realtor listened patiently, a thoughtful look on his face as Leith continued her description, then like a conjurer, had plunged his hand into a file cabinet to emerge with a picture which he handed her with an almost courtly bow.

'Give you two to one it's this place here,' he said with a self-satisfied grin, and seemed positively delighted with Leith's astonished gasp of recognition.

'I think Lady Luck had something particular in mind for you,' he chuckled a few minutes later. 'First a lottery win and then arranging to have this place on the market at just the right time. I only got the listing yesterday; haven't even got round to laying out a display card on it. Maybe now I won't have to.'

'I only wish it were true,' Leith had said. 'But I'm

sure it couldn't be within my budget, not with almost 100 acres involved.'

'Don't be a defeatist,' he replied smilingly. 'I haven't even told you the price yet.' Whereupon he'd named a figure that made Leith gasp anew.

More than she'd planned to pay ... more than she *wanted* to pay. But ... possible. Her expression must have revealed that to the realtor.

'Don't be put off too quickly,' he said. 'That's just the asking price ... it's a place to start dickering. And certainly you won't want to even consider that until you've seen the place first-hand. I don't know about your memory, but mine's not that good with two years between.'

Leith had been forced to hide a grin. There wasn't two years between sightings for her; she'd driven past the place only yesterday, both surprised and delighted to find her reaction unchanged. Whatever the magic involved, time hadn't diminished it at all.

And yet ... the price ... 'I really don't think I should even look at it,' she replied honestly. 'If it's all I imagined and I can't afford it, I'll be forlorn forever, and if it isn't what I've imagined, I should very likely be disappointed forever.'

'And if you don't look, you'll never know,' Chris Hardy replied staunchly. 'You'll have to learn to be more of a realist than that if you're planning to live in the country, Miss Larsen. I don't want to be a wet blanket, but I have to say that country living isn't for everyone and the ones that handle it best are the realists.'

'Meaning, I suppose, that it's no place for a dreamer,' Leith had replied, stubbornness firming her gaze.

'Meaning that we can be there in half an hour if we hurry,' he'd replied evasively. 'There are some aspects of the place I have to check for my files, even if it turns out you're not interested, but what can it hurt to look?'

It hadn't hurt; except that she'd immediately fallen in love with the elderly weatherboard house perched halfway up the mountain, isolated completely from all neighbours by the terrain and nestled into the riotous, overgrown garden as if it had been there forever.

Chris Hardy had been somewhat less enthusiastic, and at times had actually seemed to be trying to talk her out of even considering the purchase. The property, he said, had been allowed to run down badly, it was overgrazed in the extreme, the house was old and equally run down, the roof was in poor repair, the electrical wiring probably suspect.

Still, it had electricity and a private water supply, indoor plumbing and all the usual amenities including a huge cast-iron fireplace/heater in the lounge and a slow combustion stove hooked into the water supply.

'If you wanted to spend enough time chopping firewood you'd be able to keep the power bills down, if nothing else,' he'd said. 'I understand that during the winter the power charges are about half what they are in the summer, because the electrical hot water system isn't being used.'

None the less, he'd willingly enough walked with her around the various paddocks, pointing out the boundaries along with the generally poor condition of the fences, the good points as well as the bad.

'That entire bottom paddock needs ripping and resowing,' he'd said. 'And the top paddock, that one running over towards the mountain, isn't much better.' He continued on a running criticism, most of it making no sense at all to Leith. What did she care about the condition of the paddocks? She wasn't planning to farm the place for a living, and surely it would support the small quantities of livestock she intended to keep for her own use.

'Yes, but it isn't that simple,' was the reply. 'If you let it run down too much more, it'll cost the earth to regenerate. You've only got about forty acres of actual pasture; the rest is bush or scrub that's hardly worth developing . . .'

He continued his critique, but by this time they'd entered the house itself and Leith was too intent on looking at aspects of the interior to worry any more about the paddocks.

Certainly, she thought, the house was elderly. More than elderly; it was bordering upon being outright ancient. Much of this was explained by Chris's disclosure that it was actually two houses, one of them having been split in the distant past and each half added to one side of the original building.

And it was run down. The weatherboards were sound enough in appearance, but badly in need of a proper cleaning and painting, the galvanised iron roof was rusted and in poor repair and the interior was a hotchpotch of old and new, modern and makeshift.

And yet . . . it had a definite charm, a definite character despite the obvious crude manipulations of past handymen and some obviously not so handy.

Chris hadn't been impressed. 'Lord love us . . . I didn't realise it was this bad,' he muttered at one point. Then, catching Leith's expression, quickly amended his attitude to a slightly milder criticism. 'But, it's liveable, I suppose.'

In Leith's eyes, the house was far more than that. It was definitely liveable, and years of having to make do with minor redecorating of flats had given her an assurance with such things as paint brushes and cleaning materials. A coat of paint, she knew, would do wonders for the house both inside and out.

Besides, she was drawn to the house, drawn with an empathetic certainty that this was her place, the place she'd been seeking perhaps longer than she could now realise. It was a house that would be good to her, right for her. If she could afford it.

And, if Chris couldn't talk her out of it. Certainly he was going to try, and during the drive back to Hobart he did so with a wide range of arguments.

'And I can see that I'm wasting my breath,' he finally conceded. 'Not that I should be knocking the easiest sale I've made all year, it's just that . . .'

'. . . that you don't think I know what I'm doing,' Leith said, continuing his statement with an accuracy that brought a flush to the young realtor's face. 'Well, you may be right, but the only way I'm going to find out is to give it a go.'

She had, finally, managed to haggle the price down slightly, enough to cover her legal expenses if nothing else. And she'd negotiated some of the furniture into the deal, so that she could save something there, as well.

And now it was hers ... bought and paid for and everything. Of which, she was beginning to think, the 'everything' was the most significant word. *Everything* included the solid week of eighteen-hour days spent cleaning and painting and repainting to make just the inside of the house habitable. *Everything* meant a usually fruitless search each morning to try and discover where—if at all—the three inherited chickens had laid their eggs. *Everything* meant a continuous running battle with the cranky slow-combustion stove, a diabolical creature that seemed hell-bent on driving Leith mad as quickly as possible.

Every night, she had faithfully stoked the beast according to the directions, and every morning she'd dumped the ashes and riddled the grate. She'd also cleaned the stove inside and out, which accounted for one of her eighteen-hour days all by itself.

But no matter what she did, the stove smoked, coughing consumptive fumes from cracks and crevices that her common sense dictated shouldn't exist in the first place.

Her sojourn in the lawn chair had indeed been forced by the recalcitrant stove, and Leith had slipped into an unexpected nap while considering her next campaign in the war of nerves she seemed destined to lose.

The hound yodelled again, drawing her eye to the flashing of a small black-and-white figure that scampered down across the road and through the slightly reduced cover in the power line slash at the southern boundary. And even as she watched, the sound drifted into the gully that formed her southern boundary, the hound now lost in the scrub but its raucous voice a continuing clue to the beast's progress.

Leith considered for a moment the logic of walking down to her bottom paddock to see if the hound might emerge there, but duty grabbed at her conscience and she turned instead to return to the house and resume her ordeal with the stove.

It was nearly an hour later when she fled outside once more, smoke billowing behind her in pursuit, and squeaked with alarm as she nearly ran over the small figure of the hound as it lay sprawled in the doorway, panting heavily.

The dog was old; that was Leith's first impression. It looked to be mostly beagle, except the colour was wrong, and the white that frosted the animal's muzzle was the grizzled whiteness of old age.

She knelt to pat it, curiously unafraid as it appeared, and was rewarded with a weak swishing of the spotted tail. Dark eyes peered soulfully up at her and the dog's jowls quivered as it lurched towards her.

'Oh, you poor thing,' she cried aloud, slinging an angry glare up towards the mountain. What callous hunter would put such a burden on a dog of this age, she wondered.

The old hound's breath came in ragged, rasping bursts, and slobber dripped from its chops in great ropes. Clearly, the animal was close to exhaustion, Leith thought, and she turned back into the smoky room long enough to fill a bowl with water, which the dog accepted greedily.

'Not too much too quickly,' Leith cautioned aloud. 'You'll do yourself an injury.'

But the old hound obviously knew its limitations; after a few deep gulps, it slowed its drinking, then flopped down beside the bowl, chest heaving in great sighs.

Again, Leith glared angrily up at the invisible owner of the poor dog, and her chin firmed with determined resolution. Calling the dog to her, she picked up the bowl and led the way to the side of the yard where a previous owner had left a large, roomy dog run, complete with an enormous shade tree and a converted shed for shelter.

'In you go, old girl,' Leith coaxed, and the old dog needed little encouragement to follow the bowl of cool water into the shady run. Before the gate was shut, the hound had slumped once again into a prone position beside the bowl, dark eyes half closed as it panted heavily.

Leith returned to her assault on the stove, but her mind was only half on the job as she found herself visualising a hot verbal confrontation with the owner of the poor, exhausted dog.

'Presuming I ever get the chance,' she suddenly thought aloud, grey eyes wide with the sudden horrifying thought that the animal's owner might just choose to abandon it if the dog didn't return.

Surely that wasn't possible? Or was it? Her concentration destroyed, she found her thoughts straying up the mountain, trying to read the mind of someone she didn't know, had never met.

A glance outside reassured her only slightly. The old hound now seemed sound asleep, long ears twitching as it indulged in dreams of wallabies or rabbits still to be chased. Even when Leith stepped out through the kitchen door, the old dog didn't stir, and the faint, echoing sound of a voice calling in the hazy distance didn't seem to register with the dog either.

The sound was so far away, high up on the slopes of the mountain, that Leith couldn't determine if it was the dog's owner calling to it or some other noise, but it was sufficient to help her make up her own mind on the issue.

Clambering into the battered old utility she'd bought on her third day in Tasmania, she backed out of the driveway and then drove slowly along the road that wound twistingly around the shoulder of the mountain, pausing as she reached the track that she knew led to the source of her water supply. She'd been told that her water came from a small dam high in a rainforest ravine more than a mile from the property itself, and although Chris Hardy had checked that both her enormous storage tanks were full, he'd advised her to make regular checks on the dam and the buried pipeline that led to the tanks.

'That line's been in a long time,' he'd said, 'and there's a good bit of pressure because of the height of the dam, so there's always the risk of a break. Keep a close eye on it, and check the tanks regularly as well until you're sure how much water you're using and how quickly it's being replaced.'

A good enough excuse for the current trek, she thought, even if she knew the real reason for her journey was to check if the dog's owner really was calling or not. Chris had promised to come up one day soon and check the dam for her, which was just as well, considering she had only the vaguest idea of even where to look for it.

She drove as far along the narrow, rutted track as she dared, then halted the utility and stepped out into the almost breathtaking stillness. Here in the ravine even the incessant wind seemed muted; she could see it stirring the tops of the gum trees far above her, but down on the track there wasn't a hint of breeze.

Nor, she realised, was there any hint of the calling she'd heard from down at the house. Could she have been mistaken? Leith didn't think so, but instead of waiting she strode cautiously ahead, eyes on the ground as she sought some sign of the pipeline she supposed must run along under the track.

The road, if this crude bulldozer track should be dignified by such a description, petered out entirely just around the next bend, to be replaced by a narrow footpath that climbed precariously along the edge of the ravine to her right. But where was the water? She couldn't hear any, and dared not clamber down into the jungle of fallen logs and over-grown vegetation. She followed the path for another few steps, and was on the verge of abandoning the search when her eyes picked out a short stretch of black piping that just broke the surface of the ground ahead.

And still the path climbed! Leith struggled upward, driven now by her curiosity and the sight of a damp junction where a black plastic pipe was joined to a section of galvanised pipe that led even further upward. The pipe led off to her right, but the path led straight and she followed it until it, too, swerved to meander precariously along the fern-choked edge of the gully.

Suddenly, the sound of trickling water became obvious, and she rounded another bend to see ... no, this surely couldn't be it! Instead of the shimmering expanse of dam she'd imagined, all there was was a tiny pool of black, silt-laden sludge held back by a primitive rock wall leading from one mossy bank to the other.

All around her, the lush rainforest crouched with malevolent gloom; enormous, moss-covered tree trunks lay scattered like toothpicks among the rubble of huge, broken boulders. And through it all, a tiny stream of water trickled down to lose itself in the sludge.

Her stomach churned at the thought of having been drinking water from this source, even as her eyes confirmed the end of the pipeline emerging from the low rock wall. Another short section of pipe paralleled it, this one bent upwards and held to a fallen tree trunk by a wire tie.

'The drain?' She whispered the words, but found her voice loud in the primeval setting. Cautiously, although there seemed no logical need for caution, she stepped down to stand beside the rock wall, her eyes picking out more detail now from the shadows. Across the top of the small reservoir was a section of fine mesh wire, now choked almost solid with a mixture of silt and sodden leaves, and below that, it appeared, a stronger mesh supporting it.

Grimacing at the feel of the greasy sludge, she heaved the entire mess aside, then struggled with the drain-pipe until she had managed to get it lying in the bed of the creek.

Immediately, a stream of sludge began pouring out, and the level of goop in the reservoir began to drop quickly as well. Leith tore off sections of leafy branch and swabbed vigorously at the inside of the small enclosure, gratified to find that her efforts gradually began to clean out the accumulated debris. Elated with the success, she ignored the chill of the water and waded in, using both hands to fling aside handful after handful of the sludge, then brushing and sweeping with fresh branches until the inside of the reservoir was washed down to bare, grey rock.

It was less encouraging to find that the filter on the end of the pipeline was now revealed to be only a tight coil of fine chicken wire, equally clogged with the accumulation of sludge, but she was able to knock it clean against the downstream side of the dam and then wash it in the cleansing water that was now flowing freely through across the grey rock faces.

A few minutes more work reconnected the drain and Leith was able to sit back on the clean rock wall and watch as the trickling stream slowly refilled the dam. Only then did she realise that she'd be needing the water sooner than she might have expected. Her sneakers and jeans were black with the sludge, which had also splattered across her heavy wool shirt. Her arms and hands were relatively clean, but she could imagine what state her face and hair must be in.

'But at least it's done, and a lot more successfully than that damned stove,' she muttered to herself as she clambered back down the steep track to where she'd left the utility.

She had almost reached the truck when a faint call echoed down through the gully, too indeterminate for her to catch the words. She paused, waiting for the call to be repeated, and when it was she thought it more than possible it might be the unknown hunter calling his lost dog.

'Hoy!' she cried, cupping hands around her mouth and calling as loudly as she could in the direction from which she thought the summons had come. 'Hoy! Are you missing a dog?'

'Yes,' came the answer, floating down on the breeze from far above her.

She waited a moment, then shouted back, 'It's at the white house down the road.'

The next reply was lost to her, caught up by a vagrant breeze and distorted so that she couldn't pick out the words. And since the thought of the poor, exhausted animal had roused once again her feelings of anger at the owner, she didn't bother to seek further enlightenment.

'It's ... at ... the ... white ... house ... down ... the ... road,' she called, loudly and very slowly. 'If ... you ... want ... it ... come ... and ... get ... it!'

And without waiting for a reply, she clambered into her utility and drove off, angry thoughts raging through her mind. What did the fool want ... for her to pick the dog up and deliver it to him? No, let him come and get it, and with it a piece of her mind for letting the poor old bitch run herself into such a state.

The decision was ratified when Leith returned home and was greeted by the old hound with only the weakest flickering of a tail. The dog lay exactly as she had left it, and although more of the water had been taken, it seemed obvious the dog had little energy for anything else.

One note of encouragement was that the stove had apparently decided to behave for a while, and Leith deliberated whether to take advantage of that respite and grab a quick shower, which she now sorely needed.

'Except it would be just my luck to have that twit come looking for his dog as soon as I'm covered in soapsuds,' she said to herself, and decided to be content, for the moment, with a change of clothes and a wash.

She could have had a shower. Could, in fact, have had several; more than two hours passed and there was still no sign of the dog's owner, not even when Leith fixed herself a light snack and went to sit in the afternoon sun to eat it.

Her temper grew sharper with each passing minute, helped not a whit by the meal, and soon the dog itself began to contribute to her foul mood. Tentatively, at first, but then with growing anxiety, the animal began to howl. And it wasn't the curious yodel of a hunting hound, now, but the unremitting wail of a soul in torment.

At first, Leith thought the dog might be hungry, but even after it had greedily consumed the bowl of leftover luncheon meat she took to it the animal continued its howling, prowling now around the perimeter of the kennel.

When Leith went to speak soothingly to it, the animal stopped. But only for a moment. Staring up at her through limpid brown eyes, it waggled its tail and continued the piercing lament.

The message couldn't have been clearer: 'Let me out!'

'Well I'm sorry but you'll just have to stay here until your owner comes,' she told the dog, who responded with another tail wag and an even louder wail.

Which set the pattern for a rather one-sided conversation that continued over the next few minutes. Leith tried soft words, she tried a firm line, but the old dog's reply was consistent. It was rested now, and it wanted to go, a message it repeated in tones that grew increasingly more frantic.

'Oh, stop it,' Leith finally snapped. 'Anyone would think I was torturing you, you silly old thing.'

'Well aren't you?' The voice was so soft it could have been her subconscious replying, but Leith knew better, even as she turned to meet the flashing black eyes of the tall figure that leaned with studied casualness over her garden gate.

CHAPTER TWO

His voice was perhaps the only soft thing about him; that was what struck Leith first about the tall stranger. He seemed to have been chiseled from some dark, native stone. Black eyes, black hair, a blue-black stubble on a rigid, stubborn chin, and a tan so dark it seemed to merge with the thatch of hair on his chest.

And although he leaned casually against the gatepost, it might have been the other way round; he was so solid with muscle it could as easily have been him holding up the post.

'I ... well of course not,' Leith stammered, momentarily taken aback by the deceptive ease of his pose, by that disturbingly soft voice.

He said nothing, but those dark eyes bored into her own soft grey ones, screaming the lie at her in silent accusation. Every plane and angle of his face was rugged, rough-hewn. A strong, high forehead met the dark curliness of hair that receded slightly at the temples. The bar of eyebrows across those snapping black eyes furrowed above a high-bridged nose that flared to sensitive nostrils over a mouth that could have been broadly generous under different circumstances.

Overall, she thought, there was just too much vitality, too much sheer aliveness. And certainly too much self-assurance. He looked almost smugly superior, so much so that her earlier confusion shifted to anger at the man who would let an ageing dog work so hard under such conditions.

'You've got a nerve to accuse *me* of torture,' she snapped. 'It wasn't me that sent the poor old dog off to run herself to death ... not that I suppose you'd care anyway.'

'Oh?' It wasn't really a question, but more of a verbal

sign of the contempt he obviously felt for her opinion.
It made her all the more angry.

'Yes, *oh*,' she spat. 'And if you've come to complain
about me forcing the dog to rest, well you can just save
your breath, because I'd do the same all over again. She
was so exhausted when she arrived that I was quite
afraid for her. She was virtually dead on her feet.'

Once again he said nothing, simply stood, regarding
Leith through eyes that missed nothing as they roved
up and down her body. Not, she thought to herself, that
he'd learn much that way. The old, baggy jeans and
even baggier old sweater she wore did nothing for her
appearance and even less to advertise the shapely,
compact figure beneath them.

Her visitor suffered no such camouflage from his own
clothing. Faded jeans fit his muscular legs and thighs
like a second skin, and the equally faded bush shirt,
rolled up to the elbows and open halfway down the
front, bordered on being too small for the torso it
contained.

'Do you suppose,' he finally said, still in that soft
voice, 'that if somebody tried to tell you that you
mustn't over-exert yourself at your pottery, that it
would be dangerous for you, you wouldn't sometimes
get carried away and exhaust yourself just because of
how much you enjoy the work?'

Her surprise at his knowledge wasn't easy to hide,
but Leith fancied she managed well enough, keeping her
voice calm as she thoughtfully replied. 'I don't see what
that has to do with anything.'

'Please don't be deliberately obtuse,' he said, mouth
twisting into half a grin and one dark eyebrow raised as
if in opposition to her lie. 'You know very well what I
mean and you know equally well what the answer
would be.'

She didn't bother to deny it, but stayed silent. Let
him make the explanations, she thought; he was
obviously going to whether she argued or not.

'Of course what you really want to know,' he finally
continued, and now he revealed a grin that was

decidedly roguish, 'is how I could know about you being a potter, but of course you won't admit that, will you, Miss Larsen?'

And he chuckled throatily at her flinch. So he knew her name, too. And how much else, Leith wondered, though she determined not to give him the satisfaction of asking.

'Of course I don't know what the L stands for,' he was saying, almost musing to himself. 'So I'll have to guess. Linda? No, you're definitely not a Linda . . . Lois is too old-fashioned . . . you're hardly a Lucy, or a Lolita . . .'

'Hardly that,' she snorted, already tired of his little game. 'It's Leith, if you must know, and I suppose I might as well tell you to save you having to ask around.'

'Leith.' He spoke the name softly, curling it off his tongue and giving it a flavour, as if he were tasting it. 'Leith . . . I rather like it, I think,' he said. 'It . . . suits you.'

'I'm so glad,' Leith replied with ill-disguised sarcasm. 'And now am I expected to guess your name? Let me see,' she continued, her mind already filling with the most absurd names she could imagine. Ones like Egbert and Homer and Ichabod.

'Mace Benedict,' he replied before she could begin. 'And no, it isn't short for Mason; merely my mother's maiden name. Not an uncommon custom, although I fancy my grandfather sometimes wished his mother's family name had been something besides Arnold. I'm surprised the custom didn't die then.'

Leith giggled. She couldn't help it, despite not knowing if he was serious or not. 'It would have been a good deal worse the other way round,' she laughed, and was somehow relieved when he joined in the laughter.

Mace . . . the name suited him, especially if taken to mean a war-club, a weapon. Although he was rather regal looking, very imposing, she thought, although much less so when he laughed.

'And her name is Lucy,' he said, waving casually

towards the old dog, who raised one ear inquiringly at the sound. 'Which is one reason I'm glad yours isn't. Might get a bit confusing up on the mountain, otherwise.'

'I gather from that you intend to continue this business of letting her . . .' Leith began, but was interrupted by a definitely imperious gesture.

'It's what she loves more than anything, even food,' he said firmly. 'She's a hunter; that's what she was bred for and it's what she's done all her life. Frankly, I think if she could talk she'd tell you that when her time comes, she'd want it to be while on a hunt, not lazing the rest of her life away in a kennel.'

'That's easy for you to say,' Leith objected, but he swept her comment aside.

'It is, and there's no logic to arguing about it because I can see we're not going to agree and I've better things to do than waste my time arguing.'

'And because you obviously don't care what anybody else thinks anyway,' she muttered ungraciously, shooting him a distinctly hostile glance.

Instead of returning her hostility, he grinned. 'My dear Leith,' he said very quietly, 'if I thought you knew anything at all about the subject in question, I'd give your opinion due and proper regard. As it is, I imagine Lucy is the first dog of her type you've ever seen in your young life, although she won't be the last, presuming you continue living here, of course.'

'Well of course I'm going to continue living here. Why on earth shouldn't I?' Leith asked, her expression a mixture of suspicion and surprise at the comment.

'No particular reason, except that you don't strike me as being a country person,' he shrugged. 'And that's not a judgment; I don't believe in making snap judgments. Let's just say I'll be interested in seeing how you manage. You might surprise me by saying you were born and raised on the farm or some such thing.'

'I'm surprised you don't already know; you seem to have found it your business to check out my background,' Leith snapped in deliberate sarcasm.

'Hah! There are no secrets in the country, my girl,' he said, somehow managing to make his tone seem condescending. 'You'll find that out, in time. Everybody knows your business while appearing to mind their own, and if that sort of thing bothers you, I'd suggest you pack it in right now, because you won't change it, that I promise.'

'I don't see why it should bother me. I've nothing to hide,' she replied stubbornly.

'Then you're extremely defensive for nothing,' he grinned. 'And you're looking at this from your own viewpoint, remember. Try it the other way round. To the locals, we have a pretty young city girl, from Sydney, no less, who wins a lottery and immediately uses her winnings to buy a bolt-hole in the bush. She says she's a potter, which is really neither here nor there, but she's bought herself a farm, even if it isn't much of a farm, and she isn't—or doesn't appear to be—a farmer. Curious? Of course it is, and you can hardly blame people for being curious.'

'I'm not blaming anyone for anything,' Leith said. 'And I really don't see that it's so unusual for a person to want a little peace and quiet, a place to live in a relaxed atmosphere. Plenty of people live in the country who aren't farmers.'

'Too many,' he replied, and everything in the tone of those two words brought Leith's defences to the fore.

'Well thank you,' she snapped. 'It's nice to feel welcome.'

Only Mace Benedict seemed immune to her sarcasm. He merely grinned, revealing white, even teeth and a frightening degree of self-confidence.

'Nothing personal,' he said without apology. 'Although this place really is a classic example of what's happened to farming. The old bloke who settled this place—and it's one of the oldest properties on the mountain, I'd imagine—slaved his guts out to clear the land and plant his orchards and lay his pastures, build the houses that eventually became this one. It must have been a helluva job, but in the end he had a nice little farm. Still marginal, but something he could be proud of and he could handle, as long as his health held out.'

He looked towards the immense pine trees that shaded three paddocks at differing times of day and provided a focus for the entire layout. 'Those trees would be a hundred, maybe a hundred and fifty years old,' he said. 'Maybe less, but I remember them from when I was a boy and they were that big even then. In those days the farm took in your property and the one beside you and part of the one down past you over the ridge, if I remember right. And even then it was a viable, living farm . . . barely.'

Leith listened, making no attempt to interrupt as his black eyes lost themselves in memory. It was almost as if he were talking to himself, no longer totally aware of his audience. He told her how the original farm had been sold, subdivided, sold again and again, each time losing something in the process. It was a poignant, somehow moving story that drew her through history to her own place in the tale.

'And finally, here we are today. The place isn't a farm anymore, not really. The fences are a disgrace, the pastures are no better, you've got bracken and blackberries and probably thistles everywhere, come summer. The end result of at least ten years of neglect— and probably more to come, unless you've got a secret gold mine hidden away somewhere. It'd cost you as much as you paid for the place to bring it back to where it was at best, and it would be money down the drain, from some points of view, because in today's situation it still couldn't be a viable farm.'

'Especially,' Leith interjected, 'when it's owned by somebody who isn't a farmer.' And her voice must have registered her hurt, because Mace flashed her a glance that could only have been taken as gentle, almost compassionate.

'I didn't say that. And nobody's blaming you, nor should they. Neither am I trying to rain on your parade, because I'm sure you have strong feelings for the place or you wouldn't have bought it in the first place.'

Then he grinned, and it was very close to the shy, mischievous grin of a small child. 'Besides, who says you're not a farmer? You haven't tried, yet, and you'll have to . . . I can promise you that. You won't have any choice.'

And again that mischievous grin. 'Besides, you must be planning some degree of self-sufficiency or you wouldn't be here. You've already got fowls; that's a start.'

Leith hesitated before replying. This man, she was thinking, knew far too much. Worse, he had the facility for extrapolating from what little he did know, and she wasn't at all sure she wanted to be the subject of such conjecture.

'I hardly think a few chickens and ducks makes a farmer,' she finally said. 'And I'm not planning much beyond that.'

'Then I'd suggest you start,' Mace said, waving one bronzed hand in an expansive gesture that took in the house paddock and those adjacent. 'Because in about . . . four months' time you're going to be surrounded by grass so high you won't be able to move.'

'Oh, surely not!' He had to be kidding, Leith thought, looking around her. The paddocks were cropped so close that the bare skin of the earth below was revealed; it was impossible to imagine them covered in high grass.

Except, of course, in the house yard itself, where the grass was proper lawn grass and would obviously require mowing sooner or later. 'I had thought I might get a sheep just to keep the grass down in here,' she admitted, 'but I don't think . . .'

Mace Benedict shook his head sadly, the gesture sufficient to halt Leith in mid-sentence. 'Lesson number one,' he said. 'Sheep do not make good lawn mowers, at least not in a yard where so much time and effort has been spent on establishing shrubs and trees. Put a sheep in here, even tethered, and I don't fancy you'd like the results. Where you want your sheep is out there, in the

paddocks. And you'll need a lot more than one to even
make a dent in the grass, once spring comes. And, of
course, once you've got the boundary fences in fit shape
to hold them.'

'No,' said Leith. 'I don't know anything about sheep,
or about fencing, for that matter. And I can't afford to
fix the fences anyway, so I'll just have to take my
chances with the grass, for this year, at least.'

'And when the fire season comes and you're
surrounded by long, dry grass, you'll be taking chances
that border on the suicidal,' Mace replied gravely. And
without asking or waiting for permission, he opened the
gate and strode through. 'Come along, I think we'll
take a short stroll and see just what shape the fences *are*
in. I'd expect the paddocks closer in aren't that bad, at
least.'

Leith's involuntary gasp of protest was drowned by a
joyful yodel from Lucy, who fairly bounced against the
kennel wire as her master approached.

'No, old girl, you'll have to stay here,' Mace told the
dog in a kindly voice. 'I know what you're like; you'd
be a mile away in two minutes and I'd be getting
accused of cruelty all over again. Now, Miss Larsen,
come along and listen carefully, because this is all stuff
you're going to have to learn sooner or later, like it or
not.'

And he surged through into the house paddock,
Leith dragged behind as if in the wake of a hurricane as
he marched grimly along, eyeing the fences, the
condition of the remaining winter grass and everything
else about the property with a criticism far stronger
than that exhibited earlier by young Chris Hardy.

Leith understood only bits of what he told her, and in
any event she had so much trouble keeping up with his
long-legged stride that many of his words seemed to get
lost in the increasing spaces between them.

About the only time she got everything he was saying
was when he halted in the shade of the huge pines and
stood, hands on narrow hips, staring down at the pile of
logs on the ground. Leith had already noticed them

during her casual wanderings, and had mentally thanked an unknown benefactor for the ready supply of firewood.

'Well,' said Mace Benedict, 'it's nice to see they've left you something of value, anyway.'

'Yes,' Leith replied. 'Although I've plenty of firewood for the moment and I haven't yet bought a saw in any event. But they'll be handy later on, won't they?'

'As firewood?' And the expression in those black eyes was so outraged she cringed.

Then he shook his head as laughter rumbled up to explode from him in heaving gusts. 'Firewood ... oh, Lord, now I've heard everything. Those, my dear child, are fenceposts. Good ones, too. Mostly peppermint, fairly well split, worth ... oh, maybe $50 for the lot. And you want to burn them? Oh, I can see great things in the future for your self-sufficiency, I can ...'

'Stop it! Just stop it!' Leith cried, fighting back the tears of frustration and embarrassment. She was already striking out at him, fists clenched, her anger bubbling and frothing to the surface. How dare he laugh at her like this? How was she to know? Then she stumbled on something and was flung against him, her fists still clenched, still searching for a target as bands of iron clamped around her waist, lifting her clear of the ground and effectively halting her stumbling assault before it got going.

'Settle down ... settle down,' the voice was softly harsh in her ear, not like the burning trace of the lips that uttered those words, lips that touched at her neck, her earlobe, her throat, like a burning, fiery brand.

She could feel the muscles of his body against her as he held her close, his mighty arms almost squeezing the air from her lungs, her breasts crushed against his chest, her arms flung wide around behind his head.

And then, before she could object, resist, even think of those things, she was thumped solidly back to earth, jammed down solidly as if he were setting a post into the ground. And he was, thankfully, no longer touching her, but stepped back two paces and looking down into her angry grey eyes with a smile that made her only the angrier.

'I . . . you . . .' she spluttered, the words frothing like her anger, incapable of emerging with any sense and the more confused by his arrogant, self-contained assurance.

'Why do I have the feeling this has been too much, too fast for you?' he said with an engaging grin. 'And my fault, too. I'm sorry, Leith. I didn't intend to pick on you like this.'

And there was something in the way he said *Leith*, something so intangible but so soothing, that she found herself unable to stay angry. Worrisome, that. He was far too handsome and far, far, too charming, too well aware of how just exactly to manipulate her emotions.

'Well, I suppose I do tend to make it easy for you to laugh at me,' she replied ruefully. 'But that doesn't make it fair. After all, I've never claimed to know any of these things.'

'Just as well,' was the reply, couched in a voice that was gruff, but still friendly. Unfortunately, Leith thought, he was probably only trying to hold back further laughter at her expense.

'And nobody asked you to interfere in the first place,' she shouted. 'Besides, what difference does it make to you if I *do* burn the damn fenceposts . . . it's none of your business?'

'Waste is anybody's business, but I take your point,' he said. 'And I might point out that I have apologised once; I've no intention of doing it again. Stop being so damned defensive, woman. It doesn't become you.'

'Well that's none of your business either,' she snapped. 'So why don't you just take your dog and go? I'm sure I can manage quite well enough without you, today and in the future.'

'Are you always this temperamental?' he asked in a distinctly curious voice. 'I certainly hope not; it won't make things any easier for you if you are. And somehow I can't imagine it . . . you just don't seem the type.'

'You don't know anything about my *type*,' Leith cried. 'You've never even met me until today and you don't know anything about me, although I'm sure that won't stop you making up whatever suits you.'

'Settle down,' he cautioned. 'Nobody's setting out to make up anything, except maybe you and your built-in defensiveness. And it's *that* I don't understand. Surely you're not finding it too much for you already; you've only been here ... what ... a week? That's hardly time to draw a breath, much less let everything get you down. What's the real problem, Leith? Is it just the change in life-style, or something else?'

'It's ... nothing,' she replied evasively. How indeed *could* she explain to this supremely confident, obviously capable man that it wasn't the change in her lifestyle, not exactly. That it was a deep, inner fear that she couldn't cope despite her fondest dreams, despite her intentions? That she was feeling inadequate, as much by her inability to cope with the stove as anything else, but that his emphasis on her ignorance, her lack of rural knowledge, only served to make things worse?

'... have to take things easy, don't rush into too much, too quickly,' he was saying. 'Life in the country is very much a day-to-day thing, and while it often seems there's never enough time, you'll find eventually that there's enough, if you don't let yourself get too hassled, especially by little things.'

Leith shook her head sadly, understanding what he meant—at least in principle—but unable to admit to this handsome, overpowering man that it just wasn't that simple.

'Look at today, for instance,' he continued, ignoring her silence. 'I would have thought you'd be pleased with yourself. You came up to straighten me out about the dog, found your dam needed cleaning out—and did it! Quite a good job, too, considering you hadn't come prepared.'

Her heart soared. A compliment? That was the last thing she'd have expected from Mace Benedict. Flattering, but also just a bit frightening, suspicious.

'I ... uhm ... thank you,' she finally stammered, her eyes watching closely for something yet to come, some sting designed to remove the pleasure of the compliment.

'You're welcome,' he said with a slow smile. 'But flattery wasn't the point I was trying to make. I think you must look at that incident as typical of rural life. You can plan anything you want, organise your days to a fare-thee-well, but inevitably something will come up to throw your plans awry, and the only way to cope without going mad is to just treat each little emergency as it comes, not letting it throw you so far off stride that everything comes apart.'

'You make it sound as though planning is a waste of time in the first place,' Leith said in reply, unsure if his commentary really required an answer, but unable to halt her tongue.

'Not at all. Planning is essential if you're to progress. But in the country it's often best to remember the immortal Burns—"The best laid schemes o' mice and men, Gang aft a-gley."—and not let yourself get too upset when he proves to be right about ninety per cent of the time.'

'I shall try to remember that,' Leith sighed, making a mental note to add the Burns/Benedict philosophy to the long and growing longer list of things to be remembered. Where would it end, she wondered? The stove, alone, was enough to cope with, but first Chris and now this autocratic Mace Benedict seemed able to conjure problem after problem right from thin air. If she were to devote her energies to everything they'd mentioned just so far, she'd have no time for potting until she was old and grey.

'Of course you will,' said Mace, suddenly bringing her to the realisation she'd been thinking out loud again. Leith flushed, but he only grinned at her embarrassment. A friendly, engaging grin, devoid of the smug superiority she'd expected.

And during the rest of their fencing inspection, he seemed rather lost in thought, saying little as they strolled along, but clearly attuned to the condition of every fence post, every section of wire.

Leith trudged along with him, now silent also as she tried to see through his eyes, to feel through his powerful fingers as he occasionally pushed against a suspect post or plucked at the wire to test its strain. But for the most part, it was all she could do just to keep up with him. Mace Benedict walked with the loose, easy, swinging stride of a countryman, and he was so much taller than Leith's five-foot-five that she sometimes had almost to run to match his pace.

By the time they returned to the house and an ecstatic greeting from a now fully recovered Lucy, Leith had no hesitation about inviting Mace to stop for coffee, and she was inordinately pleased, somehow, at his easy and immediate acceptance.

Until she opened the door of the house!

She was thrust backward by a rolling smog of pungent black smoke, thrust backward into arms that lifted her and swung her easily as a child despite her bitter, angry condemnation of 'That damned stove!'

'Ah,' he said, strangely, sagely wise. 'Now that, I think, explains a great deal. Can I take it you'd never coped with a slow-combustion stove before you arrived here?'

'You may take it that I'm still not coping with the damned thing,' Leith cried, almost in tears from the combined frustration and renewed embarrassment.

Twisting free of the hands that now seemed over-sensitive to the slenderness of her waist, she folded her arms and began a slow count to ten, not the first time the stove had provoked such an exercise.

Benedict ignored her, having stepped over to fully open the back door and peer through the diminishing cloud of smoke to look at the stove. Then he walked thoughtfully around, back through the gate, and stood where he could see the thin stream of smoke issuing from the sooty black stove-pipe outside.

Leith was still fighting back tears when he strode back into the yard and bent to examine her woodpile, stifling a curse as he straightened with a chunk of nine-inch stovewood in his hand.

'Is this all you've got for firewood?' he demanded, already surveying the yard as if he somehow expected a new woodpile to appear from nowhere.

'No, there's a great pile of it over beside the fence,' she replied. 'Only . . . it's still in chunks of log and I . . . I haven't got round to buying an axe or anything yet, so . . .'

'So you've been working with this lot of rubbish; no wonder the chimney's clogged up,' he snarled, and even though she sensed that his anger was directed less at her than at some previous, perhaps unknown tenant, Leith flinched from the violence in those dark eyes.

He strode over in the direction she'd indicated, and finally stood leaning on the fence as he surveyed the enormous pile of log rounds that lay scattered untidily around several huge blocks that obviously had been used for chopping and wood splitting.

'Huhm . . . that's a bit better,' he muttered. 'There's enough here to last you most of the winter, once it's split.' Then he turned and his eye caught the old rain-water tank that lay on its side, half-full of firewood already split and ready for use.

'Better and better,' he said, shooting her a glance that as much as accused Leith of not even knowing the supply of dry, seasoned wood existed.

'I've been using that other because it was there, already stacked beside the house,' she said in a voice shrill with defensiveness. 'I . . . I didn't know there was anything wrong with it.'

'I thought we agreed you weren't to be so defensive?' was the calm, half-amused reply. 'Save your energy for what's to come, like transferring all that rubbish over here someplace to stack and season, and then shifting a great bunch of this *seasoned* stuff over by the house for you to use after we've cleaned the chimney.'

'Oh, but . . . but . . .' She got no further. Mace wasn't even listening, but had strode through the gate and towards the larger of the sheds on the property.

'Hey! Where are you going? What are you doing?' Leith cried, trotting after him. She wasn't sure if she should be angry or grateful for his take-command attitude, but she did know she couldn't let him take over without an argument.

'I'm going to see what I can find to fix the chimney,' he replied without breaking stride, or even looking back at her. 'You just get started on that woodpile, or we'll never get round to that coffee you promised.'

'Why ... you ... you autocratic so-and-so,' Leith muttered under her breath as she turned away. If Mace heard, he ignored it, and she rather thought he hadn't heard. He continued to ignore her as she struggled back and forth from woodpile to woodpile, arms aching under their burdens of good firewood and poor, totally unable to tell the difference. And, she thought, it was just as well he couldn't hear the things she muttered under her breath as she trudged backwards and forwards, backwards and forwards.

Especially when he called to her in mid-journey, using a voice that implied she should drop her load of wood and come right now!

Leith forced her aching body around to the front of the house and halted obediently where Mace stood glowering at the base of the chimney. His dark eyes were shooting thunderbolts at the structure, and his voice when he spoke was throaty with barely suppressed anger.

'You come and look at this,' he growled, 'and then start thanking your lucky stars that this old house hasn't burned down around your pretty little neck.'

All Leith could see was an opening that seemed full of cinders, but as she knelt to peer inside, Mace thrust the end of a long stick inside and showers of soot and cinders rained down from the opening.

'Plugged so close to solid it makes no difference,' he said, and shook his head in sorrowful anger. 'How anybody could let it build up that bad, I honestly can't imagine. That stove can't have worked properly for six months ... maybe longer than that.'

Which gave Leith at least some consolation. If the chimney had been clogged that long, it couldn't have been her fault. But it might as well have been her fault, for the imperious way he directed her back into the house, now relatively smoke free, and ordered her to start pushing out the slag from the inside.

'I'm off to see if I can't find the one thing we really need,' he muttered half to himself. And then to Leith, 'You haven't noticed any old pieces of chook mesh about, I don't suppose. Well, don't worry about it, I'll find something.'

Using a variety of kitchen utensils and odd bits of stick, she had the inside of the flue apparatus nearly scraped clean when he finally returned and autocratically bent to inspect her work.

'That'll do for now,' he growled. 'Now come out and keep an eye out at the bottom of this damned chimney.'

When Leith emerged from the house, it was to find Mace Benedict's boots neatly arranged at the bottom of the ancient ladder that had always leaned against the side of the house, and the man himself looming like a gigantic spectre on the roof. In his hands was a coil of rope, from which dangled what appeared to be some rusty iron wrapped in layers of chicken wire.

'This might be a bit messy, so keep well clear,' he grinned. 'Especially if the chimney starts to come down.'

Whereupon he flipped the end of the rope, casting the weight into the open top of the chimney pipe. It dropped, grating roughly during its descent, then stopped about halfway down, if Leith could judge from the sound. Enormous quantities of new slag spilled out of the opening at the bottom, but the weight remained snagged.

Mace reached up, stretching to grasp the rope at the edge of the pipe, then slowly drew up the weight and let it hang down beside the blackened pipe, obviously measuring the amount of clogged material still to be removed.

'I may have to buy you a new chimney before I'm

done with this mess,' he grinned, and flung the weight again. It roared downward more quickly, this time, coming to a halt with a thud that shook the entire structure.

'My God! You'll wreck it!' Leith shouted as he hefted the cleaning weight once more, but Mace only grinned as he flung the makeshift implement into the chimney. Again and again and again, he lifted the weight, and each time it dropped, further chunks of cinder and slag poured out on to the ground below.

Leith stood transfixed, not knowing whether to stop him—always assuming she could—or to just get out of the way in case the vibrating structure collapsed entirely under his assault.

She got no time to make up her mind. Suddenly, in a vast shower of soot and cinders, the makeshift chimney cleaner crashed through to land with a thud in the pile of debris at the base of the chimney.

Mace Benedict uttered a cry of triumph, then set about working the mass of wire back and forth through the chimney several times before replacing the chimney pot and finally descending from the galvanised iron roof.

Sitting down to tug on his boots, he grinned up at Leith, and it was the kind of grin that clearly heralded a partnership of great success.

'Now, we can see about organising some coffee,' he said. 'And a wash, which might be first on the list of priorities. How do you feel about the theory of conserving water by showering with a friend?'

And then he laughed at the expression of horror that must have crossed Leith's face. 'Is that a blush I see underneath all that soot?' he chuckled. 'You must go find a mirror; you look like a child that's been out playing in the dirt.'

'Well that's certainly a case of the pot calling the kettle black,' she countered, her composure quickly recovered. 'I couldn't be any dirtier than you!'

Which was only just true. Mace Benedict's hands, forearms and even his face showed the effects of the cleaning operation. There was soot everywhere. And when Leith did look into a mirror, she found that she was equally grimy, with a massive black smear across her forehead, her clothing black with soot and her hands so filthy they didn't look as if they'd ever come clean. If she'd needed a shower after cleaning the dam, the need was trebled now.

The need, but not the time, Leith decided. Mace Benedict appeared to have been teasing, but there was something, some inner devil behind those laughing black eyes, that made her cautiously aware that his teasing wasn't all fun. Then some inner demon of her own spoke up, and she found it all too easy to imagine taking Mace seriously, her imagination inordinately fertile when it came to thinking of sharing the shower with such a tremendously vital, compelling figure.

She found herself surreptitiously studying the strong, muscular column of his throat, the broad, rolling expanse of shoulder, the inherent, almost blatant masculinity of this first visitor to her new home. And Leith decided that she could end up being too, too attracted to the over-competent Mace Benedict. Far too attracted.

He spent the next five minutes showing her how to properly lay a fire in the combustion stove, then sluiced himself clean at the kitchen sink while Leith prepared coffee and marvelled at how the stove now functioned without any of the usual devilish antics.

With the chimney clean and a belly full of proper, seasoned firewood, the stove was behaving impeccably, almost, she thought, as if it were afraid to offend her visitor.

'I really can't thank you enough,' she said after the coffee was poured and they both were seated at the huge, old pine table that she'd inherited with the property. 'It's just ... well it's nothing short of miraculous the difference you've made with that stove.'

'The miracle is that the damned thing didn't burn this place to the ground, and you with it,' he replied, eyes narrowed as he shot the stove a venomous glance. 'It wouldn't have been the best of welcomes to your new life-style.'

Leith shivered visibly at the thought. Fire, she knew, was a major danger in a rural situation at any time, but a faulty stove in a tinder-dry, wooden house like hers would be virtually suicidal. And she hadn't known! What other things, she wondered, might exist as equally dangerous and equally unknown hazards?

She had hired an electrician to check out the wiring, and had, of course, been watchful of the recalcitrant stove, but to find now that her own ignorance had been such a threat was sobering.

'How often should I be thinking of cleaning out the entire chimney?' she asked. 'I know I must do the stove itself every week, but . . .'

'If it's working properly you shouldn't have to do more than a lick and a promise once a week,' he said. 'And the chimney's probably all right until the end of the winter, now . . . but keep a close eye on it just in case. There are usually only two things that contribute to problems with slow-combustion stoves. The most important is the wood you're burning and the other is the chimney itself, which we've now solved for the moment. Leave that rubbish wood to season until next winter, if you can. You've enough decent wood, once you've split that other stuff up, but early in the summer is the time to be cutting wood for *next* winter—so it has the entire year to season.'

And he looked at her, his eyes roving over her slim figure not in a sexual appraisal, but in the critical fashion of an artist studying the lines of a sculpture. 'And if you haven't already lined up a boyfriend, I'd suggest you make the first criterion an ability to handle a chainsaw and fencing gear,' he said, causing Leith to scowl at the implied chauvinism.

'Lining up a boyfriend, however capable, is pretty far down on my list of priorities,' she replied stoutly. 'I think it would make far more sense to learn to do these things myself—or is there some male chauvinistic rule in Tasmania that says I can't cut my own firewood just because I'm female?'

Mace didn't reply, but the half-amused look on his face served as answer enough. It did nothing to ease Leith's growing temper.

'I suppose you'd expect me to hire some *man* to construct my pottery kiln for me, too,' she demanded, 'despite the fact that I've built half-a-dozen at different times in my life—all by myself. I would point out, Mister Benedict, that being female isn't always synonymous with being helpless!'

'Just with being stubborn—and defensive,' he shrugged. 'I really do wish you'd remember that nobody's trying to pick on you.'

'Well you're doing a pretty good job without trying,' she snapped. 'And it isn't fair. At least you could give me a chance to show that I'm not totally inadequate.'

'Far from totally inadequate,' Mace retorted. 'But definitely totally argumentative and totally defensive. And,' he grinned, looking out the kitchen window at the unmistakable sound of an arriving motor vehicle, 'I think now I see why. I seem to have been far behind you on the subject of lining up boyfriends.'

Leith scrambled to her feet, eyes following his gaze. She wasn't even aware of her gasp of surprise at the sight of Chris Hardy emerging from his car, then reaching inside to draw out a chainsaw and a heavily laden tool box!

Mace Benedict's dark eyes seemed alive with accusation, or was it merely her own conscience that was reflected there? Leith knew only that no explanation could dispute the obvious—but why should she care a fig what he thought, anyway?

CHAPTER THREE

'WELL, that was quite a surprise, finding Mace Benedict here, not to mention the both of you looking like dispossessed chimney sweeps. Really, Leith, I wish you'd called me when you started having problems. I really should have checked that stove more closely . . .'

It was only the third time she had heard the refrain, but Leith mentally shut her ears, thinking that young Chris was starting to sound like a broken record. Worse, there was a mildly possessive note in his voice that she wished was not there.

It had been even more obvious some time earlier, when Chris had strode up to the gate and met Mace Benedict emerging from it. Then, Leith had seen a distinct flicker of totally unwarranted jealousy in the younger man's eyes.

They had been cordial, but it was the cordiality of two male animals, each sizing up the other as a potential opponent. That they knew each other had been immediately apparent, as had been the totally unconscious superiority exuded by Mace Benedict. On his own, Chris was an outgoing and confident personality, but beside the intense masculinity, the supreme, almost formidable character of Benedict, he virtually faded into the background, totally over-shadowed by the other man's vitality and presence.

Greetings had been exchanged, then Mace had quickly made his departure, barely giving Leith time to voice her thanks for his assistance and advice.

And his parting glance, she felt guiltily, was as full of accusation as it could be, accusing her of exactly what she'd been thinking of before his arrival, unknowing that she'd already decided it would be wrong for her to lead young Chris Hardy along, wrong to use him, to use his skills, while offering nothing in return.

It was, she was finding, a resolution easier said than done. The young realtor seemed oblivious to her attempts to reassure him that she could manage on her own, would prefer to manage on her own. And the fact that he'd found a potential rival—in his own eyes, at least—helping Leith, only made it more difficult to ease out of the situation gracefully.

In the end, she'd been forced to accept his intentions, to let him work through the remainder of the afternoon to provide an enormous pile of firewood. And then to offer him a meal, hoping that during the meal she could somehow find the right words to set him straight about the future—the *lack* of future—in their relationship.

Far easier said than done! From the outset, Chris had seemed bent on discussing Mace Benedict, and Leith had found her own curiosity too strong to resist. She hadn't prodded obviously, but certainly, she realised now, she hadn't done what she should have done, which was ban the subject entirely.

Mace Benedict, it seemed, was one of the district's largest and wealthiest landholders. He was a lawyer in Hobart, but even this busy profession didn't keep him from actively managing both the family grazing property and several others he'd acquired over the years.

And—not that Leith needed telling—he had a positive abhorrence of hobby farmers in general, resenting the waste of good agricultural land, the usual lack of management exhibited by too many small property owners.

'I have to sympathise with him,' Chris had said at one point, 'but it's something that's happening around every city in Australia and it's something that isn't going to change. And I can hardly complain about a trend that's helping me make my living, can I?'

Nor would he, Leith realised. Chris had the potential to become a growing force in the local real estate world, combining youth and charm and vitality with a single-minded dedication to his business interests. And one of those interests, although he never directly said so, must be Mace Benedict. No aspiring young realtor could afford to place himself in direct opposition to someone whose place in the community made him a force to be reckoned with.

In the rural community, Mace Benedict was just such a force. He had land, interests in virtually every facet of the livestock industry, business interests throughout Tasmania. Power! That covered it in a single word, and Chris made no secret that it was exactly that which he personally coveted.

Leith, on the other hand, held less interest in Mace Benedict's business dealings than in the sparse personal information that was forthcoming. It was no surprise to discover that the man was held to be one of the city's most eligible bachelors, nor that he moved easily through the rarified strata of Hobart's upper society.

That, somehow, was far easier to rationalise than his unexpected presence on her property, much less the apparent relish with which he'd tackled the dirty job of cleaning her chimney.

Long after she'd finally seen Chris away, indeed long after the mid-winter darkness had fallen like a shroud around her tiny house, Leith found herself wondering what had possessed Mace Benedict to so positively involve himself in her affairs, and more important, whether she must expect him to make a habit of it, as young Chris seemed bent on doing.

It wasn't likely, she decided, and ensuing days proved her right. The troublesome aspect was not being able to stop thinking about him, especially when the hounds were yodelling on the mountain as happened most weekends.

The first time that happened, Leith found to her own discomfort that her concentration was totally destroyed. She kept looking outside, always half-expecting to see Lucy dragging herself into the yard, always denying the attraction of such a visit, heralding as it might another visit from the dog's owner.

But gradually she came to know and recognise the various hound cries, and although they never failed to stir her interest, Leith forced herself to concentrate. There was too much to be done for her to waste energy wondering about a man who'd only seen her once, who'd made it clear despite his being helpful that he thought her a misplaced inhabitant on the mountain, a land waster.

Someday, perhaps, he would come to realise that she was serious about her transition to this life-style, but for the moment she must concentrate not on Mace Benedict and his chauvinistic opinions, but on her own work, her own attitudes. There was a kiln to be built, a studio to be somehow created from the ancient log-and-slab structure that had once housed dairy cattle, farm machinery and a primitive shearing shed. There was a garden, threatening to engulf the entire house yard as spring brought forth more and more blossoms, increased growth.

Life became a never-ending marathon of work as she cleared the vegetable garden, ripped the rotten plank floor from the shed she planned to use as a studio, cursed the inadequacy of the temporary facilities she had to use in the meantime. And cut firewood! Leith came to dread even the sight of the woodpile, knowing that every time she looked at it there would be a visible reminder of the one task that could never be completed, *should* never be neglected.

She bought a chainsaw, conquered her instinctive fear of the dangerous but ever-so-useful tool, and gradually became quite proficient in its use. She learned to judge her cuts, eventually making the required nine-inch wood almost instinctively, learned also to split the log rounds cleanly and easily.

From a minor landslip on the sloping top paddock, she carted load after load of sandy clay, which she packed in place of the rotten timber floor. Old planks found scattered throughout the property eventually provided shelves, and purer clay dredged from the bottom of the duck dam provided an interesting alternative to the various commercial varieties she utilised in her craft.

She assembled her small electric kiln after it finally arrived from the shipper, but despite the obvious labours required, she dreamed of a wood-fired kiln and kept an eager eye on each Saturday's Hobart *Mercury* want-ad section in search of sufficient good fire bricks. It meant driving a thirty kilometre round-trip early each Saturday morning so as to have the paper in time to investigate any possible bargain, but Leith didn't mind that.

Especially not the morning an up-dated auction sale advertisement promised a solution to her dreams—an auction that her map revealed to be only a few miles from the shop where she'd bought her newspaper! A good quantity of both ordinary and fire-bricks was on offer, and although she'd half expected to be forced into buying brand-new and therefore expensive fire-bricks, it seemed too good an opportunity to pass up.

She arrived at the site well before the earliest of potential buyers, pleased at the opportunity to wander freely among the vast quantities of merchandise contributing to the auction. It was, she thought, a relatively typical farm auction, with lots of machinery, vehicles, household goods, and the usual host of "items too numerous to mention". These included anything and everything, much of it junk but all, Leith knew from past experience, a bargain to some buyer.

Best of all, the fire-bricks on offer seemed hardly used, very much worth buying if the price stayed reasonable. It would have to be very reasonable indeed to match her budget.

As the time for the sale approached, the crowds increased until every paddock surrounding the site was jammed with row upon row of motor vehicles. Families, most of them obviously rural, predominated, and Leith didn't feel a bit out of place despite her workaday costume of jeans, sneakers and heavy bush shirt. Most of the people around her were dressed much the same, having obviously come straight from morning chores, while others looked more like city families out for a day's pleasure, and some even sported expensive, almost holiday gear.

The sale began with the more mundane sundries, things like old tyres, boxes of mingled, usually ancient auto parts and others that to Leith's eye had contained nothing but junk. The auctioneer began with an announcement about cash and credit arrangements, and Leith only half-listened until suddenly what he was saying struck home. Then she panicked!

'All terms strictly cash. Cheques or credit must be arranged with our office before bidding.' And all Leith had with her, bar the small amount of cash for petrol and lunch money, was her cheque book!

Fighting her way through the crowds, her chin firm with angry recriminations for not having had the sense to expect such a situation, she made her way to the sale's office and hurriedly stated her case.

It was no great problem, the clerk assured her, taking her name, viewing identification. Then the clerk asked for an estimate of how large Leith's cheque might be, and with the question came the oddest sensation, one that caused Leith to glance to her left at the tall, somehow familiar figure that now stood beside her.

Black eyes beneath black eyebrows bored into her own while a sensual mouth twisted into a grin that might have been friendly, but somehow seemed sinister in the extreme.

Mace Benedict! And with him, indeed so close as to be almost a part of him, the most stunningly beautiful woman Leith had ever seen. And, considering the setting, one of the most stunningly dressed.

Leith stood there, surprise having twisted her tongue into something totally unmanageable, her attention riveted not on the clerk and his question, not even on Mace Benedict, but instead on the stunning red catsuit worn so casually by his lovely, dark-haired companion.

'Well, Leith ... the man's waiting for an answer.' Mace's voice was quiet, soft, yet it seemed to boom through her head. 'Just an estimate will do; nobody's going to hold you to it,' he then continued, something like amusement flickering through his dark, all-seeing eyes.

Leith remained speechless. Confusion and something akin to sheer embarrassment raged like a whirlwind inside her skull. She heard him, understood the words, yet couldn't reply. All she could think of—and it infuriated her—was that she might as well have completed her own casual costume by wearing gumboots. And why should that matter anyway? She had no claim on Mace Benedict's attentions and didn't want one.

Then he sighed, rather heavily, she thought, and when he spoke again there was less amusement and more of what might be termed impatience in his voice.

'Well? Surely you haven't come to an auction without some sort of budget in mind? Snap out of it, girl!' And he sighed again, this time in distinct exasperation. 'What did you come to buy—if anything?'

'Bricks.' Somehow she forced that single word past her tangled tongue; somehow she met his eyes.

'Bricks.' He repeated the word almost as if he didn't believe her . . . or didn't care. Leith wanted to expand, to explain, but her mouth betrayed her by merely opening and shutting without a sound, as if she were gasping for air.

He reached past her, lifting the sale catalogue and quickly skimming through the list of offerings. 'Firebricks . . . or just the others?' he demanded, having found the appropriate entry.

'Both.' She was recovering; that word escaped with a minimum of problems. But she couldn't yet manage more, so Leith wisely shut her mouth. Mace Benedict didn't seem to notice.

'Right,' he said, turning to the clerk and naming a figure that was five times what she could possibly pay. 'And if it's more, I'll stand behind it,' he continued, then turned away without another word and before Leith could even think to thank him, he and his lovely companion were filtering into the crowd.

All that remained to Leith was half a comment, uttered in silky, velvet-smooth tones: '. . . was that

urchin?' and Mace Benedict's 'sort of a neighbour'
reply.

Her immediate reaction to rush after them, to
somehow find the appropriate words to thank Mace for
his intervention, was thwarted by their direction. He
was making for the tractors and heavy equipment
section, and a sideways glance revealed the young
auctioneer was almost at the pile of bricks Leith had
coveted.

Coveted? It would perhaps go no further than that, if
Mace's price judgment was to be considered. Leith
would no sooner pay that price than fly to the moon,
even if she did think he might well believe she could be
carried away by auction fever into paying more for old
bricks than even new ones were worth.

He probably would think such a thing, too, she
mused, but so what? If he was interested he'd have
ample opportunity to find out that she wasn't quite *that*
gullible.

By the time the sale reached the bricks, Leith had
recovered most of her composure, if not her confidence.
The prices offered for the last few lots seemed, to her,
quite out of all logic, with some items selling for a
pittance and others going for more than they'd have
been worth new.

And she found it difficult to concentrate. The brief
encounter with Mace Benedict and his lovely companion
should not, Leith thought, have so thoroughly upset
her. Should not—but it had, and she couldn't deny it
even to herself. Not disputing the man's undeniable
attractiveness, it simply made no sense.

Unless, she thought, it was the unavoidable mental
comparison between her own rough-and-ready working
garb and the ultra-chic, high-fashion tone of the outfit
worn by Mace's lovely, dark-haired companion. Leith
might be living in the bush, but she had lost none of her
femininity, or hoped she hadn't. Perhaps that was it—
the simple feminine desire to look her best, to be seen in
at least a reasonably favourable light when compared
with a potential rival.

'Rival?' Leith muttered the word aloud, then had to stifle a giggle. Some rival *she* made, dressed like an unemployed farm labourer and with a life-style that Mace Benedict firmly and obviously disapproved of. And besides, she wasn't interested in being a rival. The dark-haired woman could have Mace Benedict and welcome to him; Leith would settle for her pottery and her independence.

And with that thought firmly established in her mind, she concentrated on the approaching auctioneer and the bidding for the bricks she was interested in.

The ordinary bricks were sold first, and from the beginning Leith knew she wasn't even to have a look-in. The prices started just below her budget figure and quickly rose to almost exactly the reckoning Mace Benedict had calculated in the auction offices.

Leith was vaguely disappointed, but hardly surprised. The weathering and character in old bricks frequently gave them a value out of all proportion, often, as in this case, a value beyond what the same bricks would cost new. The principle couldn't—she hoped—apply to the second-hand fire bricks, and it was these which interested her more than the others. Leith had already determined that if necessary she could use mud bricks for the exterior of her kiln, provided she could get enough fire bricks for the double lining she wanted.

Provided! It was a large question, especially considering the crowd that jammed around the brick pile. Everybody, it seemed, was interested in the bricks. Leith sighed audibly, then firmed her chin in determination. She would stick to her budget no matter what; to pay more than she'd planned would be a folly, a false economy in the long run.

The bidding began, and her hopes soared at the early lack of interest. She stayed silent as the auctioneer began to pull down the price, seeking a starting bid from which he could force the increases.

The first bid took her momentarily by surprise, but hers was the third, then the fifth and—even more surprising—final bid. And the fire bricks were hers at less than half the price she'd expected! Leith was jubilant, and the more so when she turned to find Mace Benedict nodding in a gesture that could only have been approval.

It wasn't until she'd paid for the bricks and begun the finicky task of loading them into the back of her utility that she realised Mace's companion had also been watching the bidding, and her look had registered anything *but* approval. It had been, Leith decided, an almost hostile glare.

And that was ridiculous. Surely the gorgeous brunette didn't view Leith as some sort of competition? Not Leith dressed as she was, that was for sure. Even at her best, and she had to admit she was relatively attractive, Leith couldn't see herself matching the elegant, sultry loveliness of the brunette.

Smiling to herself, she shrugged off the mental discussion and concentrated on getting the bricks loaded properly. Having got such a bargain, she didn't fancy having half the bricks destroyed by the jouncing they would surely get on the rough gravel track up the mountain.

'Do you really expect to get that bucket of bolts home with a load like that on it?'

The voice came from behind her as Leith lowered the final brick into the bed of the truck, and she was startled so much she almost dropped it. No mistaking that voice, so soft and yet so vibrantly alive.

'I don't see why not,' she replied cautiously, turning to look up into black, unsmiling eyes. 'I'll have to take it pretty slow, of course, but old Matilda isn't built for speed anyway.'

'Matilda,' said Mace Benedict with a scowl of distaste, 'is hardly built for anything, except perhaps the wrecking yard.'

'That's not true,' Leith snapped angrily. How dare he insult her vehicle? 'She might be a trifle elderly, but she's a perfectly good truck for what I need, not that it's any of your business anyway.'

'It'll be everybody's business if the thing collapses in

a heap of broken bricks out on the highway,' he retorted, voice still soft. 'And as for getting up the mountain . . .'

'I will manage, thank you,' Leith interjected, staunchly hanging on to her temper.

And even as she faced up to Mace's queries, her mind was divided, a portion of it wandering the crowd around them, seeking out the man's apparently absent companion. Where was the gorgeous brunette in the red catsuit, Leith wondered, half speculating that the woman might have already tired of the hot dustiness of the auction paddock, the swarming crowds and raucous noises.

'What I was going to suggest,' he continued, blithely ignoring the evidence of her determination, 'is that I know several people here who live out your way and who have, uhm, decent trucks . . . at least trucks rather more capable than yours of handling such a load. I could arrange for the delivery of your bricks that way, and you'd still have them home today.'

Logic said he was right, and some other, less definable feeling made her want to accept, want to show that she wasn't averse to the help of a neighbour. And yet, she found herself refusing, albeit politely. Stubbornness, one of her largest faults by her own admission, had slipped in to take charge of her attitudes.

'Oh, no, really . . . I'll be able to manage quite well enough by myself,' she said. 'It's very good of you, but . . .'

'But you're determined to be stubbornly self-sufficient,' he growled, eyes flashing with scarce-subdued hostility. 'Or is it just me, I wonder? You won't seem to be quite so adamant in refusing help from young Hardy.'

'I'm not adamant about refusing help from anyone,' Leith rejoined. 'When I need it. And for this, I don't need help so I don't wish to make myself a nuisance to anyone, if you don't mind.'

'Nobody said anything about you being a nuisance,'

he replied, voice once again soft, yet somehow vibrant with held-back emotion.

'That's easy enough for you to say,' she retorted. 'But we can't say as much for whoever you'd planned to rope into transporting my bricks, can we?'

'*We* couldn't, perhaps, but *I* certainly could,' was the grim reply. 'Since it would have been me doing the delivering . . . or at least my truck. There'll be a load going right past your place later today, and another tomorrow, for that matter.'

'Well thank you anyway, but I'm sure I can manage,' Leith said before he could continue, before the urge to accept grew too strong to be resisted. Then, from the corner of her eye, she caught the flash of something brilliantly red approaching, and some demon caught her tongue, making it snap out with, 'Besides, I'm sure you'll be too busy today to worry about playing delivery boy.'

The look that that gained her was caustic, a blistering, scorching flash of black eyes before he turned to stride off, greeting the approaching woman in red with a cheerful remark and ignoring Leith as if she'd never even existed.

Leith didn't wait. Leaping into the now-loaded utility, she started it with a savage turn of the ignition key and lurched into a slow, careful retreat from the rough-textured paddock, feeling her elderly truck shudder at the weight of the load like an overloaded beast of burden.

Driving with extreme care, alert to every pothole, every change in the surface of the bitumen road ahead of her, she slowly made her way towards home, thankful there would be only the three-mile gravel track up the mountain to cause her problems.

Almost from the outset, she found herself wishing she had accepted Mace's offer; the elderly utility was clearly overloaded to the point of being dangerous and by the time Leith reached Brighton her wrists ached from steering the cumbersome machine.

She was also feeling rather light-headed, a condition

she put down to the lack of anything in her stomach since dinner the night before. It took no encouragement at all to swing into the parking lot of the Brighton pub as hunger took over Matilda's direction.

Well-known and justly renowned for its counter meals, the pub was crowded, and most of the crowd seemed to have come from the auction. Leith splurged her remaining cash on a large shandy and a hearty meal of roast pork, sharing a table with a party of older women who chattered on as if oblivious to her presence.

She wasn't really interested in their conversation until a remark from one of them caught her attention; after that she shamelessly eavesdropped.

'. . . that red outfit. Of all the things to wear to an auction sale,' was the first remark, and Leith paid great attention to what followed.

'Well, we all know Madeline DeMers. And she's always been famous for her flamboyance,' said another of the party.

'Perhaps, but there's such a thing as going too far,' was the reply. 'What could she possibly be trying to accomplish by such a performance?'

'That's obvious enough; although why she should think Mace Benedict would be impressed by such an exhibition I can't imagine. Still, she's been after him for years and maybe this was some sort of last-ditch try.'

'Oh, hardly that,' said another. 'I think it's just that Madeline loves to be noticed.'

'Being with Mace Benedict *is* being noticed,' was the catty reply. 'Wearing an outfit like that is rather gilding the lily, I should say.'

'More like belling the cat,' purred yet another of the women, and Leith had to hide a chuckle that the others could enjoy openly.

The rest of the conversation was only slightly less vituperative, and Leith learned that Madeline DeMers was the sole daughter of a prominent Hobart family, that she had been expected to marry Mace Benedict for years, was still expected to marry him, and that if and

when she did, it would be considered a great shame by
virtually every other woman who knew the man.

Not, she quickly decided, a terribly popular lady, this
Madeline of the stunning red catsuit. In fairness,
however, Leith had to admit that Mace Benedict must
be considered quite a catch indeed.

Certainly, from what had been said, he was well-liked
and equally well respected in the district. Even Chris
Hardy, while trying not over-hard to conceal his
opinion of Mace as a possible contender for Leith's
own attention, had made no bones about the man's
popularity.

She thought back to their encounters of that
morning, easily recalling the mental picture of Mace
Benedict, tall and erect in casual but expensive clothes,
clearly the landholder, the countryman, the leader of
other men. Perhaps she had been too hasty in refusing
his neighbourly offer, she thought, not that it mattered
a great deal. What was done was done, and perhaps in
the long run better this way. Leith had no desire to
encourage further relations with Mace Benedict,
however impressive he might be, and certainly the
exhibitionist Madeline DeMers wouldn't welcome any
interest on Leith's part.

Or anyone else's, Leith thought as she returned to her
truck for the fifteen-kilometre journey home. There had
definitely been a very proprietorial air about the dark-
haired woman, flamboyant outfit notwithstanding. It
was surprising Mace had been allowed sufficient rein to
allow his approach about transportation for Leith's
bricks.

'Now who's being catty?' she queried to herself
aloud, and frowned at her rear-view-mirror image.
Then she chuckled happily and discarded all thoughts
of Mace Benedict and his red-clad lady. What could it
matter to Leith anyway? She had her bargain bricks,
her fairytale cottage and a life-style she was coming to
enjoy more each day. It was doubtful, Leith decided, if
Madeline DeMers could say as much, even with her
social standing and startling clothes sense.

And for some reason, now even the contrast between their clothing added to Leith's good mood. She drove cautiously but not that slowly home, Matilda lumbering up the rough gravel track of the final bit of journey without even a hint of the problems Mace Benedict had so arrogantly predicted.

'And *that* to you, too,' Leith scoffed aloud as she rounded the final bend and turned into the driveway to her farm.

Leith spent the next week laboriously creating mud bricks for the outside of her kiln, and the week after that labouring long hours at her wheel, her attention so fixed on her work that she had no time to think of Mace Benedict or anyone else. Creativity seemed enhanced by the bucolic surroundings as she gradually slid into a routine. She found herself doing more work, and—most important—better work than ever before. She experimented with new glazes in the electric kiln while her mud bricks dried in the paddock, experimented with new shapes, new textures, in the clay creations she planned for the wood-fired kiln when it was ready.

There were no surprise visits from Mace Benedict, for which she thought she was thankful, and she had also managed, with considerable subtlety, to make Chris understand that while she welcomed his own occasional visits, she had no romantic inclinations and didn't want any.

One day each week had been devoted to making the rounds of craft shops, and she was gradually building a list of outlets that were more than pleased to handle her work. In some respects, it was easier to sell in Tasmania, where a thriving tourist industry was closely allied to crafts and craftsmen, aided considerably by the Crafts Council of Tasmania. Leith had found the council officers most helpful, and had joined the organisation as a matter of course.

She soon found that her Sydney reputation had followed her south; her pottery began to sell at increasingly good prices, and the demand from her craft shop contacts increased as winter gave way to the coming of spring and the tourist season that seemed to burgeon with the riotous spring flowers that followed the daffodils into being.

And at home, there was more than flowers. Mace Benedict's comments about grass began to echo in Leith's ears as she found the house paddock, especially, becoming thicker and thicker with new grass.

As the next week passed, she deliberately walked throughout her paddocks, startled now at the amount of grass and the speed with which it seemed to be growing. The following Monday, she drove off early to attend the weekly stock sales at Bridgewater and gain some idea of what it might cost her to get some sheep.

What had Mace Benedict said? She should get two-tooths, hoggets, that was it. 'Something with a bit of sense,' he'd said. Well, she wasn't going to buy anything at all on this particular visit, Leith thought, but it wouldn't do any harm to look.

It was her first visit to a stock sale, and at first she was stunned by the noise, the bustling activity as thousands of sheep, from tiny lambs to large, burly, curling horned rams were deftly shifted from pen to pen by tall, quick-moving men and well-trained dogs.

Enormous stock trucks rolled up, loaded with sheep, and in minutes were rolling away again empty, their passengers merged into a growing sea of grey-white wool.

There were sheep in full wool, sheep with no wool at all, their coats cropped close and shining white from the fresh shearing, sheep of every size and description. Most, Leith thought, looked rather bewildered by it all, even as she, herself, was.

She wandered down the alleyways between the pens, listening to the talk around her and looking, trying to make sense of what she heard. And her confusion must have been obvious, because within minutes a tall, lean, bearded man paused in his brisk stride to ask if he could assist her in any way.

'Well,' she said cautiously, 'I was sort of thinking I might like to buy some sheep, only I don't know anything about them and . . .'

Under his prompting—it turned out he was a buyer for one of the meatworks—Leith explained her situation in some detail, unable to help thinking it must sound rather ridiculous to this man, who bought sheep in the hundreds and thousands. All she really wanted, all she could afford, might be five or six.

But if he thought her mad, the man was far too polite to reveal it. Instead, he pointed towards the far corner of the yards and suggested she ought to find a few pens there with only five or six sheep in them.

'If you find anything you like, come and let me know and I'll see about getting them for you,' he said, then strode away again on his business.

Leith did as directed, but after surveying the few small pens she was really none the wiser. The sheep all looked much the same, and at close quarters appeared rather larger than she'd expected. She was working her way back towards the front of the yards, more than tempted to give it up as a bad job, when she spied a small pen she hadn't noticed earlier.

And this one seemed the answer to her problem! It held just six animals, all fat and sleek looking, with appealing black faces and legs that gave them a ludicrous expression, she thought. They looked friendly, cheerful, and she could almost imagine them gambolling happily around on her paddocks.

With some difficulty, she located her adviser and brought him to check on the pen for her. The sheep were, he said, Suffolk cross-breds, probably ten or twelve weeks old and in very good condition. 'You'll have to bid against the butchers for that lot,' he said, 'but you might get them for, oh, eight, nine dollars each.'

'That young?' she said. 'But would they do what I want, like eat off the grass on ten acres or so?' Mace Benedict's advice about getting older, more sensible sheep niggled in the back of her mind, but Leith hadn't seen any older sheep that appealed; these six definitely did.

'If you don't eat them first,' was the reply. 'And very tasty they'd be, too.'

She stood looking at the lambs after he'd gone, mentally computing their cost as they stared back at her with tragi-comic expressions.

Their dark eyes seemed to plead with her to buy them, and the man's comments about them being perfect for the butchering trade seemed to ring in her conscience, drowning out entirely the 'just looking' attitude she'd arrived with. But should she? Suddenly it seemed a very big decision indeed. She knew nothing about sheep, and in truth didn't really want to get involved with them. But ... there was that grass; she had to do something about that.

'What are you dreaming about—lamb chops or lawnmowers?' Leith found the all-too-familiar voice easy to identify despite the hubbub around her.

'Lawnmowers,' she replied, turning to meet the black-eyed gaze of Mace Benedict and bracing herself for the expected criticism of her choice. She mentally kicked herself for not expecting to run into him here, especially considering she'd just decided to ignore his advice entirely.

Mace was dressed in faded work clothing, the khaki colouring pale against the depth of his sun tan, and Leith found herself wondering idly what he'd look like dressed up, wearing the business suit his work as a lawyer must demand. Then she shook herself. What a thing to be thinking, especially here and now, when he was working and thinking like a stockman.

He didn't immediately, however, begin the expected criticism. Instead, he stepped into the pen with the lambs, his powerful, sensitive hands running over them as he checked their condition.

'I wouldn't give more than ten dollars each for them,' he said then, 'and you might be lucky enough to get them for eight.'

Beyond him, the auction was in progress, the auctioneers moving along catwalks above the pens and disposing of the sheep with what seemed to Leith to be incredible speed. She saw Mace glance in that direction, then he turned back to speak to her again.

'Are you going to stand here and guard them, or come and watch the sale?' he asked with a grin. 'They won't fly away, you know.'

He strode towards the area where the sale was in progress, and Leith trailed along with him, absurdly conscious suddenly that, as now seemed inevitable, Mace Benedict was seeing her dressed as she did for work, in faded jeans, a heavy and hardly flattering bush shirt and worn gumboots.

Her memory too readily supplied an image of the glamorous Madeline DeMers, resplendent in that vibrant red catsuit, and Leith shuddered at the comparison. Then she squared her shoulders and marched strongly behind Mace. What could it possibly matter what she looked like? He didn't look at her with any sexual interest, merely as a unique and not overly welcome neighbour.

And, she thought, probably as a nuisance as well. They didn't talk as the sale progressed down the line of pens. Indeed, talk would have been difficult if not impossible in the riot of noise that surrounded them. Instead, both concentrated on the sheep being offered and the bidding for them, and for the first time, Leith realised what the lengthy drought that encompassed most of Tasmania's sheep country was doing to prices.

She saw what appeared to be prime lambs going for ludicrously small prices, especially when she considered their cost as meat in the butchers' windows, and heard the muttering of those around them as the prices fluctuated throughout a range that could only be considered low.

When the sale came to *her* pen, she bid cautiously, ever-conscious of Mace's commanding presence beside her, and struggled to withhold her obvious glee when she found herself owning the lambs at only $7 each. But she couldn't hide it completely, and was pleasantly surprised when she turned to find Mace smiling down at her.

'That was well done,' he said. 'Now how about some coffee? It'll be some time yet before you can arrange to load them; it's best to let the large buyers get their mobs shifted first.'

When they entered the small snack bar at the sale yards, where Mace nodded greetings to almost everyone present, Leith once again felt herself becoming highly self-conscious about her attire. Just being in Mace's company was enough to draw curious attention, and she felt like her position as a stranger added to it.

Mace brought their coffees, along with a small plate of sandwiches and cakes, then sat in contemplative silence for some time before he spoke.

'I gather from the size of your flock that you intend to let the rest of your pastures go for this year,' he finally said. 'If it stays dry, and I think we must expect that, those half-dozen lambs should just about keep the grass under control in the three paddocks just around the house.'

'That's the part that worries me the most,' Leith replied seriously, thankful he didn't seem to be assaulting her choice of lambs as against the older sheep he'd recommended earlier.

'So what will you do about the rest—let them go to hay?'

'I . . . uhm . . . don't know yet,' she replied honestly. She hadn't, in fact, even thought about the possibility of haying her paddocks, and from the look on Mace's face, he knew it.

For a long moment he sipped at his coffee, dark eyes roving across Leith's face, dipping to inspect her hands, with their unkempt nails and the callouses that came from both her pottery work and the general, day-to-day effort of keeping her property going.

'Tell me,' he finally said in a voice that was suspiciously soft, even more suspiciously enticing, 'do you know anything about farming . . . anything at all?'

'I'm . . . learning,' she hedged, not quite able to meet his eyes.

'From young Hardy, no doubt,' he snorted, not bothering to hide the contempt in his voice.

'Chris was raised on a property,' Leith retorted, not

intending to leap to Chris's defence, but unable to resist. What business of Mace Benedict's was it, anyway?

'And got out of it as soon as he could,' Mace replied evenly, his eyes revealing that he'd deliberately baited Leith and now felt amused that she'd so readily bitten. Then, in an abrupt change of subject, he said, 'How's the stove going, all right?'

'Very well, thank you,' she replied, struggling to conceal just how easily he could throw her off balance with his verbal jousting.

'And the potting? Or do you find time for it much?'

'Plenty of time,' she said, puzzled. What was he getting at? Was this some back-handed criticism about the condition of her property, or a referral to the number of times—four, actually—that Chris had come to visit before she made it clear she was really too busy for a lot of socialising?

Leith thought for an instant that perhaps she ought to straighten Mace Benedict out once and for all about Chris Hardy's place in her life, but as quickly as the thought occurred, she discarded it. What business was it of his? He certainly had no claim on her time; she'd not seen him, except at the auction, since that first time he'd come in search of his wandering dog.

'How's Lucy?' she countered, then. And immediately sensed that Mace knew immediately she was only trying to steer the talk to safer ground.

'Lucy's fine, although not getting any younger or better behaved,' he replied. 'She's really starting to slow down now, though. Doesn't stray nearly as far.'

Which, Leith thought, was a typically unsubtle way of telling her he still allowed the dog to hunt, despite the obvious risk that one day she simply wouldn't be able to return.

'You haven't got a dog yourself, yet?' he asked then, so casually she was certain he already knew the negative answer. 'You might need one, now you're setting up as a sheep farmer.'

Leith couldn't help chuckling. 'I hardly think six

lambs constitutes a sheep farm, much less justifying a dog,' she replied. 'Although, I wouldn't mind having one just for the company, sometimes.'

'The isolation getting to you?' Again, it was one of those questions that neither deserved nor demanded a reply. She ignored it, noting as she did so that Mace seemed to have expected her to do exactly that.

Suddenly she felt confined, almost trapped by this man's uncanny ability to follow her thinking, almost to read her mind. She wanted to get away, yet conversely she was loath to flee, to admit the effect he was having on her. It was with great relief that she noticed an approaching stranger, obviously intent on gaining Mace's attentions.

'I think I'd best go and straighten out the financial side of my sheep farming,' Leith said hurriedly, anxious to leave the newcomer a clear field. 'Thank you for the coffee and all.'

'Anytime,' was the terse reply. He didn't bother to ask if she could manage her flock without help; there were plenty of sales yard staff around in any event, as both of them knew.

Two of the younger staff were more than helpful, driving the lambs to a loading ramp between the huge flocks intended for the big transport vans, and helping to place the lambs into the makeshift stock racks in the back of Matilda.

Leith didn't see Mace again; he wasn't anywhere handy when the loading was done, so she took that absence as an omen and drove slowly homeward, both relieved and vaguely disappointed.

There, she turned the lambs out into the house paddock and buried herself in the pottery for the rest of the afternoon, trying vainly to focus her attention on her work, yet always seeing that black, black hair and those snapping dark eyes lurking on the edges of her consciousness with sinister intent.

She ate a cold, quick supper, then went to check on her lambs just as dusk began to settle from behind the mountain. They seemed peaceful enough, if rather nervous of her, so she didn't push them.

Leith went to bed shortly after dark, but her night was restless, uncomfortably so. Part of the reason was the recurrent images of Mace Benedict and her own chagrin at his ability to get under her skin, but mostly she slept badly because of the lambs.

They, she suspected, didn't sleep at all. Throughout the night she found herself waking unexpectedly, half-consciously listening for their plaintive baaas. They seemed to be thoroughly exploring their new home; she would hear them over near the pine trees one minute, and then, seemingly only moments later, down near the tea-tree scrub or over by the shed-cum-pottery.

She wondered several times if she mightn't have been wiser to confine them at first in one of the small paddocks on either side of the house, but always discarded the suggestion, at least until morning. Somehow she couldn't imagine herself out rounding up sheep in her nightgown, presuming she could even see them.

By the time proper sleep came, it was already early morning, and as a result she overslept, finding herself still tired when she finally awoke to find the sun well up ahead of her.

From the barnyard, the subdued squawking of ducks and chickens, all waiting for their morning feed, became a strident command when the birds saw Leith open the door and emerge in hastily donned jeans, boots and jumper.

But one sound was missing, and she needed only to scan the paddocks to know with sinking heart that her tiny flock of lambs had gone walkabout during the night!

Hurriedly, she flung the chook food out to the waiting birds, then even more hurriedly trotted down the track that led to the bottom paddock, hoping—expecting—with each step to see woolly figures emerging from the scrub or grazing quietly somewhere just out of present vision.

Within a few minutes, however, she had to face the awful truth. Her lambs not only had left the house paddock, they'd left her property entirely! The big question was—where?

CHAPTER FOUR

THE lambs helped Leith to find them, eventually, but there all co-operation ended. Using her ears, she located one lamb deep in a bushy corner of the bottom paddock, and after an hour of frantic chasing she managed to manoeuvre the creature into one of the small paddocks next to the house.

Then it was off to find the others, who finally made known their presence through lonely, plaintive cries into the wind, announcing that they'd managed to scramble through three different fences already and were highly indignant at being separated from Leith's neighbours' sheep by a fence so stoutly made the creatures couldn't get through.

Leith stood, panting from her earlier exertions, and regarded this masterpiece of fencing with a new respect. Unless her lambs had learned to fly, which she seriously doubted, they had already managed astonishing escapes through fences that looked nearly as formidable— although her own fences, she had to admit, could have presented few problems.

By the time she'd regained her breath, it became obvious that taking the wanderers home again would prove a difficult task indeed. There were gates she could open, but none existed on the boundary between the properties, so how could she push the errant sheep back through on to her own land?

Retracing her steps along the fencelines, she finally found one section that could be propped open to let the sheep through, so having done so, she returned to begin driving them home. It was a task, she found all too quickly, that was far more easily planned than executed.

At first it seemed easy enough. She circled round the lambs and slowly shifted them up against the fenceline, then down it until they'd passed the open gates and were approaching the break in the fence on her own boundary. But then the fun began!

It was as if they'd read her mind! One instant the five lambs were ambling happily along an old track between the scrub and the fence—the next they'd sighted the propped section and taken immediate subversive action, breaking back into the bush and circling around Leith at a quick trot she couldn't possibly match.

By the time she caught up with them, thanking her lucky stars she'd at least shut all the intervening gates, they were back at the last gate involved in the trek, obviously still intent on joining her neighbour's flock.

She circled them again, again began the slow trek back to where she hoped she might direct them through the fence and at least back on to her own property.

And again, within feet of the opened fence, they turned right instead of left and gambolled through the bush with a thoroughly-frazzled Leith in angry pursuit.

And it happened again . . . and again . . . and again . . . She eventually went back to the house and scattered a trail of chook pellets along the intended route, but the lambs joyfully ignored this, as they did the jumper she hung on a branch in a bid to spook them from their usual turning point.

Throughout the performances, their baaas, which during the night had seemed to Leith to be plaintive and lonely, seemed to take on a laughing, mocking tone. It was as if the beasts were in cahoots with the ever-efficient Mace Benedict, who'd undoubtedly be rolling on the ground in laughter if he could only see her, Leith thought.

Her own pace lagged as she struggled back and forth, up hill and down, but the recalcitrant lambs seemed to grow fresher, more alert, almost as if they were enjoying the game.

She thought at one point that perhaps she might capture the lone lamb in the small paddock next to the house, somehow lead him to the others and pray they'd follow him back again. Fat chance! She quickly found that the lone lamb was even spookier than the others, and she'd be a week catching him . . . if ever.

Leith carried on the struggle until noon, when common sense and sheer exhaustion forced her to reconsider. It was obvious she could follow the stray lambs back and forth forever without improving her chance of getting them where she wanted them. Clearly it was time to throw off her pride and independence and seek help.

She returned to the house, climbed stiffly into Matilda, and drove down to her neighbour's gate, planning her apologies and tale of woe as she went. The whole thing was a task she did not relish, and yet, what choice had she? She couldn't leave the lambs running loose—especially on this same neighbour's property. And she certainly couldn't get them home by herself, she'd already proven that.

And yet . . . to appeal for help from someone she'd never met, had indeed actually avoided meeting in her own bid for independence and solitude . . . Still, it had to be done, she thought, and as she drove into their yard she steeled herself for the ordeal.

Her preparation was mostly wasted, because Leith was greeted warmly by George and Helen, who emerged from their home to call off an elderly yellow Labrador who threatened to eat Leith if she dared emerge from her truck.

'You'd best come and have coffee before we do anything,' Helen said. 'Frankly, you look as if you need it.' Helen was a short, stout woman with merry bright eyes and a generous smile, while her husband had the unruly good looks and flamboyant cheerfulness of some wild Irish rebel, all flashing grin and bright blue eyes and curly black hair.

Neither of them, surprisingly, seemed to find it at all unusual for Leith's first visit to be one seeking help; she was immediately welcome.

Leith quickly relaxed in their friendly company, so much so that she had to struggle at times to keep from letting her frustration over the wandering lambs drive her into tears.

Under Helen's probing questions, she revealed she hadn't had breakfast, much less lunch, and moments later was presented with a plate so heaped with food she had to fight to get through half of it. George, in the meantime, had walked off to inspect the lamb situation personally, and he returned just as Leith finished her second coffee, announcing that it would be considerably easier to drive the lambs down into his own yards and truck them home from there.

'They'll settle down after a few days,' he said with a broad grin. 'Right now they're lonely and looking for their mothers that's all. What you should have bought, by rights, was two-tooths, or even older ... something with a bit of sense.'

Leith almost choked as he said it, the words almost identical to those of Mace Benedict and the context of the advice even more so. Then, catching Helen's inquisitive glance, she laughed aloud and told them the reason for her laughter.

'Good advice, but it would be, from Mace,' was the response, issued in tones that avoided any reprimand or hint of it. Helen's next words, however, were drowned by a roar of challenge from the dog outside, and Helen peered out the window, then turned and said, 'Well, speak of the devil.'

Leith could have sunk through the floor. No question what that comment meant; especially when the tall, black-haired figure strode through the door and greeted them all with a broad smile.

But the warmth of the greeting was dispelled—at least for Leith—by his very first words. 'Hi there, Little Bo Peep,' he grinned, obviously taking in the situation at a glance. 'And tell me, how long did it take for your little flock to escape?'

'About as long as it would take to say: Should have bought two-tooths, or something with a bit of sense,' Leith snapped, trying to subdue the rising of her anger and humiliation with humour and knowing she was doing a very poor job of it.

And they all laughed, though Leith fancied there was

something besides humour in the gleaming dark eyes of Mace Benedict. Sadistic enjoyment, more than likely, she thought, and hated him for it.

'Don't pick on the child, Mace,' Helen cautioned with a shaking of one forefinger. 'She'll learn in time, and it's hardly a crisis anyway. They could have run in with our sheep for months before George even noticed.'

'That's not the point and she knows it as well as you do, Helen,' Mace replied, obviously unconcerned by the threatening finger. And he was, Leith thought, only too right.

But if she was subdued by his justifiable indignation, clearly Helen was not. 'Oh, piffle,' the older woman snapped. 'Your problem, Mace Benedict, is that you expect too much of people. Now if I were you, I'd look at a girl as pretty as Leith and give her credit for trying, not jump on her for a little mistake that doesn't mean anything.'

'Chauvinist!' Mace cried in mock horror, drawing a small grin even from Leith. 'If I'd said that you'd both be on to me for pure, undiluted male chauvinist piggery, if you'll pardon the expression, being pig-farmers. But you say it, Helen, and it almost seems acceptable. Only I wonder what Little . . . uhm . . . Miss Larsen thinks.'

'I think I'd like to capture my errant lambs and take them home,' said Leith, who had flinched almost visibly at such obvious match-making. 'And next time I'll try to take more notice of people's advice, because I truly do hate to make a nuisance of myself.'

Unfortunately, Mace Benedict was right, she thought. She'd ignored good advice, genuine advice, and now she must pay the consequences, but that didn't have to mean being subjected to abuse from anyone, or—much worse—blatant match-making.

'Right,' said Mace, shooting her a glance that could have meant anything. He and George then shared a brief discussion about the best means of shifting the lambs, Mace having brought along a sheep dog, which both agreed would make the task considerably easier.

Easier! Compared to Leith's morning of frustration and torture, it was indeed easier. Pathetically so. It took she and the two men only five minutes to have the sheep from their new-found freedom to one of George's small yards. The dog did most of the work. Then the men stepped in, handling the sheep with sure confidence as they caught them up by the hind legs and gently loaded them into Leith's truck for their second journey *home*.

But it wasn't to be as easy to release Leith from what now seemed almost a conspiracy to have her thrown together with Mace Benedict. Now that the sheep had been caught, nothing would have it but that all of them should pause for yet another cup of coffee before Leith could make her escape, and when they'd finished that, she could hardly refuse an invitation to inspect the piggery.

'It's one of the most modern in the state, from all functional viewpoints,' Mace told her as they walked down the long track that linked the home and stockyards with the long set of concrete block buildings which housed several hundred pigs of all sizes.

George and Helen explained that they kept various of their animals on free range, with only the breeding sows and piglets under intensive housing. The buildings held a variety of pens, all scrupulously clean and positively swarming with grunting, squealing pigs. In various outdoor pens, larger animals swarmed to greet their owners, snuffling through the wire as if in genuine friendliness.

Her hosts apologised for the smell, which they said many people tended to find offensive, but Leith didn't find it so at all. All she noticed was the obvious care and affection lavished on the animals, and she caught Mace Benedict's obvious approval of the way the property was being operated.

In fact, much as she hated to admit it even to herself, she was far more aware of Mace than of any piggy odour throughout their tour of inspection. He loomed tall beside her, never touching her and yet somehow able to tune himself in to her in such a way that she was totally aware of his presence, alert to his every word, his every gesture.

But finally, thankfully, the time came when she could decently make her farewells and depart. Only not, it seemed, with any freedom from this man who so easily confused her emotions, provoking responses she both hated and enjoyed.

'I'll just follow along behind,' he said casually after Leith had clambered into Matilda's seat. 'I've brought you up a couple of old ewes, nice steady old girls that'll settle down your lambs until they've decided where home is.'

'Oh, but . . .' She got no further. George and Helen both chimed in their praise for the proposal, saying that if Mace hadn't brought his older ewes along they'd have insisted on providing a couple of their own as a steadying influence for the young, motherless lambs. It was, she quickly realised, a typical example of good advice well meant, and Leith knew she'd best take her own advice and accept graciously.

'Well . . . thank you; thank you very much,' she said then, determined not to be shown up as being stubbornly foolish yet again.

Mace merely nodded, but his dark eyes flashed something that might have been approval, or might have been something quite entirely different, Leith thought.

When they arrived back at her property, he insisted on another quick check of the fencing before any animals were released, and suggested one of the small paddocks immediately beside the house.

'You could keep this lot there for a month with no worries,' he said, and then shift them to the other side for another month. By then they'll be well-and-truly settled down, and you can put them back into the house paddock without having to worry every minute where they'll get to.'

'That,' Leith said honestly enough, 'would be a blessed relief.'

'I'm sure it would be; you won't get much potting done if you have to spend all your time chasing sheep around the countryside,' Mace said with a grin. 'Now come and show me what you've done with all those bargain bricks.'

Self-consciously proud, she led him to the converted shed and spent the next half-hour answering surprisingly pointed questions about her work and the efforts she'd been making to get herself properly set up.

Perhaps the best part was his knowledgeable appreciation of the artistry involved in her craft. He knew what he liked, but even those pieces which obviously didn't strike his fancy were looked at for their good points and the effects she had been trying to achieve.

'I can hardly wait until the mud bricks are totally cured, so that I can start with the wood-fired kiln,' she found herself saying. 'It's much more work, but from everything I've seen the results can be worth it.'

'Hard work doesn't seem to bother you much,' was the unexpectedly complimentary reply, and Leith found herself flushing slightly with pleasure.

'The hard work hasn't really started, yet,' she replied. 'Someday I'd like to build an entire studio from mud bricks; that's when the really hard work will come.'

'I should think so,' Mace agreed, then soured the agreement by adding, 'especially as I imagine you'll start with the intention of doing it all by yourself.'

'Do you have something against independence?' Leith retorted, slightly annoyed by something in his tone. 'Surely it's better than being a burden.'

'I have nothing whatsoever against independence, except when it gets carried to extremes,' was the unperturbed reply. 'And of course I'm not suggesting you should have to run to someone else for help with every little thing you try; it's just that in some circumstances, a little neighbourliness can go a long way, and be good for all concerned. I'd have thought today should have shown you that.'

'What today did was make me feel really stupid,'

Leith replied. 'Not that I can expect you to understand what it must feel like having to beg help from neighbours you've never even met.'

'And whose fault was that? Certainly not George and Helen's, young lady. They're the best kind of neighbours anyone could ask for; help anyone, and yet certainly polite enough so that they didn't intrude on your privacy—and won't!'

'They are really nice people. I couldn't agree more,' Leith replied.

'Well I'm glad you noticed that much, anyway,' Mace said, dark eyes darker with seriousness. 'And now that you have met them, I hope you'll try to maintain some sort of relationship, even if it's no more than waving when you pass them on the road. Just remember that they're the kind of people who enjoy helping others, and they'd be hurt if they found you were needing help and didn't ask.'

'Oh . . . oooooh!' Leith groaned. 'Don't you see that's just the problem. Of course they're wonderful people and of course they'd help me if I needed it, the same as you've done. But what about me? What can I do to help *them*? Or doesn't your neighbourliness policy extend to returning favours?'

'Ah,' he nodded wisely. 'So that's it. You don't like feeling indebted and because you can't see any way of returning help or favours you'd rather just struggle along on your own, carrying your burdens and being strictly independent, not to mention antisocial. And I suppose when somebody does you dirty you run around screaming about an eye for an eye and all that. Very biblical, but not realistic, dear Leith. Also neither pleasant nor productive.'

'That isn't the case and well you know it,' Leith snapped in reply. 'It's just that . . . oh, well, maybe you're right; I *don't* like feeling indebted.'

'Well, I'm glad to see your aversion to being helped isn't just confined to *me*,' Mace said, locking her eyes with his own. 'Although I certainly can't help feeling that you especiallydon'tfancybeingindebtedwhereI'mconcerned.'

And now he was so close, his presence almost overwhelming. Leith couldn't help herself from shrinking back slightly, half her instincts tugging her closer to him while the more sensible half retreated in alarm from the sheer physical attraction.

'I . . . well, perhaps,' she admitted, not meeting his eyes, afraid to meet them for fear of what she might reveal through her own. But then her back was against the door of the shed and there was nowhere further to retreat, yet still his presence seemed to loom above her, his intense masculinity like a tangible aura that wanted to draw her in, envelop her.

'And do you think that's such a horrible debt? A couple of hours' work on your chimney, the loan of a couple of old sheep?'

His voice had the soft harshness of raw silk, soothing and yet subtly abrasive. Leith didn't look up until one of his fingers chucked softly under her chin, forcing her head up gently until she had no choice but to meet his eyes.

'Are you afraid of me?' And the question was real, uttered with a concern so genuine she couldn't take offence. His fingers caressed her throat, moving down into the hollow above her breasts and then lifting again, never threatening, somehow, and yet so . . . so tantalisingly gentle that she shivered beneath his touch.

'Not . . . afraid,' she whispered. 'Just . . . just . . .'

'Cautious?' And she saw the glint of laughter in those alluring black eyes as his lips bent to hers, touching them only briefly and again without any trace of threat. Then he stepped away.

Away, no longer touching her, yet holding with her eyes as if she were nailed to the floor, as if there was a collar around her neck keeping her backed against the wall. And on her lips the taste of him, lingering like an elusive perfume. Leith felt weak at the knees, her entire body trembled from the force of the emotions that welled up inside her. Only her mouth still worked.

'And what was that all about?' she said in a ragged yet forceful voice.

'Just a little confirmation that perhaps you're wise to be ... cautious,' he grinned, tormenting her with the mockery she could see in his eyes, the satisfaction in the quirk of his lips. He was so damnably self-assured!

A tiny shiver lifted from her toes, growing to become a full-scale shudder by the time it reached her shoulders. Leith sobbed in a deep breath, steadying herself as she tired to control the growing anger at his mockery.

'Well just so long as you weren't entertaining any silly ideas about how I should pay my debts,' she snarled, hoping to give an impression of a fierceness she certainly didn't feel.

He only laughed. 'I thought we'd already settled that one,' Mace said. 'And after the work that went into fixing that chimney, I rather fancy my idea of sharing a shower more than your implied offer of just a kiss.'

And then he was close to her again, his mouth reaching for her lips, his fingers gently touching at her waist as he drew her against him. 'Mind you,' he murmured, 'everything has to start somewhere.'

Leith had no chance to resist. His lips claimed her in such a casual and yet self-assured fashion that there was no question of refusal, even if her body hadn't betrayed her by immediately responding to his touch.

Her mouth parted beneath the gentle assault of his lips, her body slid easily into the closeness his hands demanded, her breasts crushed against his muscular chest, her thighs feeling the warmth of his as he drew her closer.

She felt her breasts tauten against him, the nipples swelling to throb against his chest, and it was as if another mind controlled her arms, drawing them around his neck to pull his mouth tighter against her own, bringing all of him closer and closer.

Beneath her fingers she could feel the crisp hair at the nape of his neck, the rigid strength of his neck muscles. Deep in her throat a moan of pleasure rose, matching the harsh breathing of this man whose entire body seemed to draw her like a magnet, whose lips so perfectly fitted her own.

Leith felt his hands moving, the fingers flexing into the small of her back, tracing intricate, delightful designs along the curve of her buttocks, then up the nubbles of her spine as if on a keyboard of pleasure. She sighed more deeply as surrender conquered the modicum of common sense that still stirred somewhere inside her, and when his fingers lifted the edge of her jumper to caress the bare skin beneath, her body shifted itself to ease his access.

Then his fingertips were like quicksilver against her breasts, both icy cold and hot as the devil's breath, yet always, always rising in their ability to heighten her desire, lift her emotions and send her passions spiraling ever-upward.

Leith's fingers strayed on their own journey, down the column of his iron neck, into the curling chest hair and along the washboard of strong, heaving muscles as she freed his chest from the constriction of his shirt.

This is madness, cried her mind, and the words were somehow echoed inside her ears as his lips traced a passage of rapture matched only by the one his fingers created beneath her jumper. Then the words came again, and there was no resistance when she pulled back, for the first time listening to the harshness of his voice as he uttered the words himself.

And it was over. Or, thought Leith, as over as it could ever be, as over as memory would allow it to be.

'Now that,' said a voice like velvet, 'was rather more than I think either of us bargained for.'

'Oh, for God's sake don't apologise,' cried Leith, fighting for control, holding back desperately against the tears and shaking inside her, the fear that wasn't fear, but more of a heightened, frightening awareness of her own sexuality.

'Apologise? I should certainly hope not,' he said in a voice still ragged with his own diminishing passion. 'There are some things, dear Leith, that can only be insulted by apologies. And that, I fancy, would definitely be one of them.'

She looked up to find him smiling, but it wasn't the

expected smile of the conqueror, nor the smirk of a self-satisfied, self-indulgent male egotist. It was ... just friendly, rather warm and open and pleasant. And certainly not apologetic.

If he was aware of the trauma building like a volcano inside Leith—and he must be aware of it, she thought—he gave no indication at all. Nor did he try to touch her again, as if sensing that his tiniest touch was alone enough to send her screaming into shock at the strength of her own emotions.

'What say you show me your daffodils,' he said instead, in a total change of subject, a total removal from the thread of tension that linked the two of them like an iron chain. 'I wouldn't be at all surprised to find you've got a fair few of the old-fashioned double types here, and perhaps when they're done blooming you might spare me a few bulbs for the garden at home. Mum used to have some, but they disappeared in one of the renovations, somehow, and I know she'd love it if I could persuade you to part with a few.'

Almost before Leith could reply, he'd stepped through the doorway of the pottery, and stood holding the door for her, politely, almost distantly, as if deliberately giving her the chance of refusal.

'Yes,' she said, following him outside to a sunshine brighter than any she'd ever seen. 'Yes, of course.'

Most of her daffodils had already begun to wane, but by searching the masses behind the barn and then strolling silently up to the even larger clumps above the duck dam, they were able to identify several clumps of the type Mace had mentioned, and Leith wrapped short bits of barley string around the best of them to be sure of later identification.

'You won't want to mess with them now, of course,' Mace said, his voice a curious mixture now of intimacy and strangeness. 'But when they're all finished blooming and safe to dig up ...'

How was it possible, Leith thought, barely listening to his voice, that having been—even for such a short time—so close, they could now be so apart, could now walk together almost as strangers? His earlier words, 'afraid; caution' seemed now so irrelevant and yet so alive with warning.

He was ahead of her, his long strides carrying him with that typical countryman's speed, when the image of Madeline DeMers in that bold, exhibitionist catsuit suddenly sprang into Leith's mind, and she paused to lean against a fence post as tears rushed up from inside and a dreadful feeling of futility washed up with them.

How could she possibly compete with such a woman? No longer any question of whether she wanted to; Mace Benedict had branded her with his kisses as surely as he might eartag one of his lambs. The problem, Leith had to admit, was that she could just as easily end up on the spit! Certainly he didn't have any other intentions for her, not with a lifetime commitment to the beautiful, dark-haired socialite.

She caught her breath, reached out to grab for composure, then was following close to him again without a sign of the trauma that cried in torment inside her. It was a totally controlled Leith who offered coffee when they got back to the house, an even more controlled Mace Benedict who politely refused, now seeming as anxious to be gone as a tiny part of her wanted him to be.

And when he did leave, it was with a cheerful wave and a smile, with not a hint of apology, not a hint of the spectre he'd unleashed.

Leith stood in the yard for what seemed like an hour after he'd driven off, her eyes on her lambs and their older custodians, but her mind back in the pottery shed, reliving each delight of his kisses, each paradise of his touch. But finally she returned into the house and made coffee for herself, drinking it with—for the first time since she'd moved to her home beneath the mountain—an almost genuine loneliness.

The next two weeks were hell. She looked at the lambs, and thought of him, looked at the daffodils, and thought of him even more. She tried to bury herself in her work, but his face seemed attuned to her thoughts, his features now fixed in her touch. Instead of the conventional—and most important, saleable—pottery she'd usually done, she found herself toying with other things, usually facial features, the beginnings of a bust that saw Mace's features emerging from the raw, untutored clay.

Her hands seemed suddenly able to work without conscious direction, sculpting and moulding the pliant clay while her mind was far away, and Leith emerged from a particularly lengthy reverie one day to find that she had very nearly completed a particularly vicious effigy, a curiously excellent mingling of Mace's handsome features with the prick-eared, curly-tailed figure of a piglet.

And at that moment her honest humour took over, allowing her to see the ridiculousness of her intro-spectiveness, the release her fingers had provided. It took only a bit of work, then, to turn the effigy into one slightly less demonic, slightly more cute. A genuine Mace Benedict male chauvinist piggy bank, she thought with a chortle of delight.

Helen and George also thought so, when she drove down two days later to deliver the piggy bank as a present and stay for coffee and a chat.

At first Leith had thought they'd missed the likeness, but George sat shaking his head with held-in laughter while his wife cast Leith a look that showed she saw even more in the caricature than Leith might have intended.

'It's lovely, Leith, it really is,' Helen said. 'Really though, you should be giving it to Mace, even though I fancy you'd want a bit of room to run, afterwards.'

'More than a bit of room,' her husband chimed in. 'I don't reckon you could run far enough or fast enough, did Mace Benedict decide to take offence.'

'Well then perhaps we should just keep it a joke between ourselves,' Leith replied, trying to hide her second thoughts on the matter. 'Because the last thing I want is Mace Benedict chasing me for any reason.'

Liar! Her own conscience and Helen's piercing glance

both shouted the accusation, but neither, thankfully, said it aloud. And even when Leith asked for and obtained directions to Mace Benedict's property, after explaining about the daffodil bulbs she wanted to deliver, Helen merely raised one eyebrow in speculation as she provided the information.

At home later that day, Leith remained unsure if she ought to act on the directions or not. She had little inclination to meet Mace's mother, but she fancied it would be less of an ordeal than meeting the man himself. And if she timed her visit for the following Monday, when he should be busy at the stock sales, she could easily deliver the bulbs and be gone again without having to meet him.

By the appointed Monday, she was even less certain, but determined during her light breakfast that she must do it, and she would. Somehow, Leith felt, it might help her exorcise the feelings that still raged inside her, might help her remove the feeling of futility, hopelessness, and most of all return her rather damaged pride.

She could, and would show that he didn't matter, that his kisses had meant nothing, had not affected her at all. It would be a lie, but so long as only she knew that, the purpose would be served and she could somehow then manage to ease him completely out of her existence.

Her first sight of Mace's home was almost enough to make Leith turn back immediately. The homestead of native sandstone was immense and immaculately kept, tucked back in against a ridge and surrounded by greenery. All the fences were white-painted and everything screamed out a tale of long and excellent management and upkeep.

As, indeed, did the woman who stepped out on to the long verandah as Leith drove in. She was tall, though not nearly so tall as Mace himself, but she carried herself in the same self-confident fashion and in the lines of a still-beautiful face and snowy hair were such strong hereditary traits that her identity was unmistakeable.

'Well, I wondered when we'd have the pleasure of meeting,' she cried without benefit of formal greeting. And as Leith stepped uncertainly from Matilda, the sack of daffodil bulbs in her hand, 'and you've brought the bulbs Mace promised me. Oh, how thoughtful of you to bring them yourself. If I'd had to wait for him to remember it might have been next spring before I saw them.'

Which set the tone for what seemed to Leith to be one of the most extraordinary hours of her young life. It took no imagination to see where Mace Benedict got his self-assurance and boldness from; his mother was, if anything, even more so. But the real surprise was how much Fiona Benedict knew about Leith, her property, her plans, and seemingly everything else about her.

'I envy you in a way,' Mrs Benedict said at one point. 'So young and so much to learn. It was different for me; I was just as young, and probably knew even less of rural life than you do, but then I was married and had Mace's father to guide me, so of course it was much, much easier. I wonder if he ever realised how often I wished that I could just be allowed to learn by my own mistakes, and in my own time, as you're doing.'

'Well in that respect I fear your son takes after his father,' Leith astonished herself by saying. 'Except that really I feel he'd rather I wasn't here at all, wasting good farming land and all that.'

'Oh, that's just because his list of priorities starts and ends with the land,' said her hostess. 'His father was just the same ... and his grandfather, from the little I knew of him. Not, I suppose, that it makes his autocratic attitudes any easier to take.'

'Not at all,' Leith smiled. 'But I must admit that he's been very helpful, as well.'

'And so he should be,' Fiona Benedict snorted. 'You couldn't possibly be any worse than the last person who owned that property. At least you've got the excuse of not knowing any better; he was a farmer, supposedly, and he let the place go something horrible. A land-wrecker, that's what the man was.'

'Well I'm afraid I'm not doing so very much to improve it, at least not yet,' Leith said. 'Even if I did know what to do, I couldn't afford it, and I don't expect I will be able to afford it, not for some time at least.'

Fiona smiled, and there was something sad in her smile, something that spoke of times past, opportunities missed, perhaps. 'Time is the least of problems at your age, my child,' she said then. 'You just see that my son's high-handed ways don't upset you. Stand up to him as you have been doing, and if he doesn't like it, then throw him off the property and go it your own way.'

Leith had to laugh at the idea of her throwing Mace Benedict anywhere. 'I doubt if I could even lift him, much less throw him,' she chuckled, 'but I do get your point.'

'I'm sure you do,' was the reply. 'You've shown a remarkable degree of courage and common sense for your age, Leith. You've bought a good property, or at least what could be made into a good property once again with a bit of work. You've got good neighbours and you've obviously got a taste for hard work. You'll make out, never fear.'

As Mrs Benedict saw her to the door, Leith found herself with a renewed sense of purpose, a firmer sense of her own values, and she stepped down off the wide verandah feeling truly at peace with the world.

The conversation with Mace Benedict's mother had somehow put her own life back into perspective. There no longer seemed any reason to deny—at least to herself—the immense physical attraction she felt for the man. She wouldn't admit that there might be more to it than that, but whatever might be involved, she now felt able to cope, if not, as his mother had suggested, to exactly throw him off the property.

She reached Matilda and was turning to wave to Mrs Benedict when a small red sports car skidded into the drive in a flurry of scattered gravel and slewed to a halt almost bumper-to-bumper with Leith's elderly utility.

The sudden arrival caused Leith to flinch visibly, but she managed to refrain from leaping for cover, and when the occupant of the sports car emerged Leith was able to meet the hostile dark eyes with no visible fear in her own eyes.

'I remember you; the urchin from the auction,' said Madeline DeMers with a smile as cold as the grave. Her eyes raked up and down Leith's own slender figure, noting with apparent satisfaction the contrast between Leith's clean but utilitarian clothing and her own stylish pant suit.

But behind the surface politeness, questions screamed for answers, and Leith didn't need to be much of a mind reader to know that Madeline's curiosity was shrieking silently, demanding to know what Leith was doing there, what possible threat could be involved to Madeline's position and plans.

'Do you always find it necessary to drive like a madwoman?' Fiona Benedict's voice was calm and quiet, but there was steel beneath the softness and the eyes that greeted her newest visitor seemed, at least to Leith, to be chillingly cold. Certainly there was none of the openhanded greeting she herself had received.

Madeline, however, seemed not to even notice the icy comment. She glanced at her hostess, but when she replied it was with a casualness that suggested she didn't think the older woman's comment worthy of reply.

'Where's Mace?' she demanded almost petulantly. 'He was supposed to meet me for lunch, and I've been to the saleyards and everybody said he'd gone. I expected he'd be here.'

Mrs Benedict gave no indication of recognising the rudeness. 'I take it you've met Miss Larsen?' she asked quietly, then went on to finish introductions that drew only hostile nods from both participants.

'He hasn't 'phoned or anything?' Madeline demanded then, making it doubly certain that Leith knew her own importance was negligible where the dark-haired girl was concerned.

'My son is not in the habit of burdening me with his every move,' was the chilling reply, and Leith suddenly had the impression that even if Mace had telephoned, the information wouldn't be passed on except under his express instructions. There was no love lost between Fiona Benedict and Madeline DeMers, but only the older woman was subtle enough to keep an icy dignity about her.

Still, Leith thought, it was none of her business. All she really wanted was to get away from the tension, and she was about to speak up with a final departure when the rumble of yet another vehicle arriving forestalled any such move. All she could do was stand there, her earlier ebullience gone like wind-driven cloud, as Mace Benedict stepped from his truck, eyes roving across the faces of the three women and a vaguely quizzical look flitting across his dark eyes before he spoke.

'Well, this is well organised. I've just come from your place, Leith; so you've saved me a return trip.' And then, to his mother, 'I expect she's brought you the daffodil bulbs, and you've told her it would have been next year if you'd waited for me to remember, Mum. Well you can take it back, because I'd have brought them today if Leith had been home.'

But it was for Madeline that his greeting seemed, to Leith's ears, warmest of all. 'Hullo, possum,' he said in tones oozing emotion. 'You've been tearing up my driveway again with that little red horror of a car.'

There was gruffness in his voice, but it was obviously faked. And certainly it didn't slow down Madeline's rush to throw herself into his arms, her pouting mouth eagerly upraised for his kiss of welcome.

'My foot slipped, that's all,' she explained, and her dark eyes flashed from Mace's mother to Leith and back again as if daring them to speak up against the blatant lie. When neither did, she flashed a quick, triumphant grin, then focussed her attention solely on Mace.

'You were going to take me to lunch, remember, and you weren't at the saleyard so I came on here. I expected you'd be changing already, so you'll have to hurry or we'll be late.'

'I said I'd take you to lunch if I had time, and today, dear Madeline, I'm afraid I don't,' Mace corrected gently. 'So if being late worries you, best be off with you, because I've got some business back at the saleyards. The only reason I'm home is that I had to find a place to stow this, seeing as Leith wasn't home to take charge personally.'

And reaching into the passenger side of his vehicle, he emerged an instant later with a small, wriggling bundle beneath one arm.

'Just as well you're here; you can take her home with you now,' he said, handing the pup to Leith in a ceremonious gesture. 'Her name's "Snap", she's half Smithfield and half blue cattle dog, and by the time she's grown up enough to work sheep, you might even have enough to keep her busy.'

'Oh ... but ...' Leith didn't know what to say, and whatever she might have come up with was forestalled by a long pink tongue that insisted on trying to wash her face for her. Not quite a baby, the pup was about four months old, and the strangest looking apparition Leith had ever seen.

From the sheepdog parent, it had a woolly face reminiscent of an Airedale terrier, but its body was a muddle of silver, blue and cream ticking from the cattle dog side. Two curiously flopping, black-brown ears gave the pup a comical expression that was totally endearing.

Madeline's expression was anything but endearing. 'My goodness what a scrubby looking little beast,' she sneered, shooting Leith a purely venomous glare.

But Leith, who had fallen in love with the wriggling little terror at first lick, ignored her. 'I think she's lovely,' she spluttered past the puppy kisses. 'And I think we'll get along just fine; thank you, Mace, very much.'

'You're most welcome,' he said with a grin. 'Both her parents were workers, so there's at least a chance she might be, and if nothing else she'll be good company and a good guard dog when she's a bit older.'

'I think she'll be wonderful company,' Leith said, inwardly grinning at the hostility Madeline was revealing. She was half tempted to stay, if only for the enjoyment of being spiteful, but common sense said no, and instead she made her farewells and drove sedately out of the yard with the pup perched happily in the passenger seat beside her.

Both Mace and his mother waved at her departure, but Madeline, as she had rather expected, only glared after Leith with an expression that was an almost comical mixture of hostility and relief.

That alone was sufficient to rekindle Leith's feeling of well-being. How ridiculous, she thought, for the dark-haired woman to become so obviously hostile over so little. And yet, it was strangely . . . well . . . satisfying, in a way, to know that despite the difference in their clothing and lifestyles she could still put up some show of competition, even if it wasn't at all what she'd intended.

Once home, she spent the next hour or so playing with Snap, laughing at the clumsy puppy antics and wondering where on earth Mace could have found such a comical, affectionate little beast. And why? It was in fact that question she was pondering when a growl from her pup announced the arrival of a visitor. And a very unexpected one it was, too, speeding up the rough gravel track in the tiny red sports car!

CHAPTER FIVE

'I've come to apologise for being rude.'

Whatever else Madeline DeMers might have been expected to say, and certainly Leith hadn't had much chance to even speculate on the reason for the visit, this was the most unlikely.

'I ... hardly think it warrants an apology,' she replied carefully, her attention divided between the tall figure at her gate and the small growling bundle at her feet. Snap was obviously convinced she ought to be charging out to eat this unwelcome visitor, and while Leith might privately agree with the concept, she daren't allow the pup to have the opportunity.

'Mace thinks so.' And the reasoning became abundantly clear, as did the look of hatred that crept through with the unexpected admission.

Leith was astounded, though she forced herself not to show it. She wasn't all that surprised that Mace had found Madeline's behaviour rude, but that he would go so far as to suggest a personal apology ... that was truly astonishing—if true.

'Well then I think he must have misunderstood then, don't you?' she replied calmly. In truth, she thought nothing of the kind. On second thought, it seemed less and less likely that Mace Benedict would have ordered any such apology from his lady friend; Madeline was here for some other reason, even if Leith couldn't imagine what it might be. Curiosity, perhaps? Or just taking the first opportunity to assess what she might imagine to be the opposition.

'Have you known Mace long?' The question wasn't entirely unexpected, but still Leith had to fish for exactly the right words to answer. She could almost, she thought, enjoy this little verbal battle.

'I wouldn't say that I know him at all,' she replied.

'We're . . . sort of neighbours; that's all.'

'There must be more to it than that, if he went to all that trouble to find you that . . . that dog,' Madeline replied sulkily, shooting a hostile glance at the still-growling Snap.

'I didn't know he'd gone to any great amount of trouble,' Leith said. 'I had rather imagined he'd just run across it somewhere and remembered me saying I wouldn't mind having a dog, that's all.'

'Oh, and just when did you tell him that?' Madeline seemed to be getting more and more sure of herself, and her assertiveness showed up with increased rudeness.

'He stopped in to see my neighbours down the hill not so long ago when I was there,' Leith replied noncommittally, then surged forward to a more positive position. 'Why? Does it matter?'

'Oh . . . uhm . . . no, I suppose not,' Madeline replied, retreating to a more cautious approach in the face of Leith's directness. And whatever else she might have been planning to say was, thankfully, forestalled by the arrival of Helen.

Typically, Madeline didn't wait to be introduced or anything like that. Instead, she muttered something about having to go now, and was inside her sports car almost before Helen could emerge from the farm truck in which she'd arrived.

'Well, I hope I didn't disrupt anything important,' Helen said when she reached the gate and had turned to watch the red car squealing away from the drive. 'I just came to see how you were getting along with your new pup.'

'But . . . oh, I suppose there's no logic to asking how you know about it so soon,' Leith laughed. 'I know . . . there are no secrets in the country.'

'Not ever a one,' was the equally humorous reply. 'Especially not with a certain un-named male chauvinist piglet scouring the country for the last fortnight in search of a pup. Doesn't take word long to get around.

'Oh, come now. I'm sure he wasn't advertising who he wanted it for.'

Helen laughed. 'Well he'd hardly be wanting it for himself, would he? Not when he's got a kennel full of the top working sheepdogs in the state. The way I heard it, he specifically went looking for a dog that had a bit of personality and, well, a bit of blue heeler blood as well. Something that would grow up to be a bit of a guard dog.'

Leith glanced down at Snap, who now lay sprawled out beneath the nectarine tree, sleeping in the boneless slump of an exhausted puppy. 'Some watchdog,' she said, 'although she certainly would have taken a piece out of Miss Madeline fancy-pants, if I'd let her. Maybe she has some proper watchdog attitudes at that.'

'Reasonable judgment, anyway,' her friend replied. 'Now all that's to be seen is if she'll work sheep, and it'll be a while before you can find that out; she's a bit young yet.'

The two women were sitting over coffee before Helen cautiously raised the topic Leith thought might be the real reason for the unexpected visit. 'What did you think of old Mrs Benedict?' Helen asked with characteristic directness. No subtle fishing, no beating round the bush; just the blunt question.

'I thought she was lovely,' Leith replied. 'Really a nice person. Although,' she added with a hesitant grin, 'I can see where her son gets some of his self-confidence from.'

Helen chuckled happily. 'Self-confidence? By that I assume you mean his ability to take over and get things done—*his* way! But yes, he seems to have inherited most of his good points from his mother, and it's just as well because his father was a proper bastard, from all I've heard. Mace is just as tough, but he lacks the cold-bloodedness. He really does care about people.'

'Provided,' Leith interjected, 'they're proper farmers and don't go about wasting their land.'

'Of course,' Helen said, as if there could be no other proper attitude.

'Yes,' Leith said. 'Which tends to make me just a bit suspicious of his motives in giving me this puppy and

... oh, and everything he's done. He doesn't think much of my being here; I'm not a proper farmer and really, Helen, I never will be, so why does he bother with me at all? And don't say it's just because I'm a new girl in the district, because I'm sure Mace Benedict isn't short of feminine company, even if we ignore Madeline DeMers.'

'Rather difficult, that. Ignoring dear Miss DeMers, I mean. And I wouldn't go downgrading your own attractiveness, Leith. Maybe he's got a thing for blondes.'

'Oh ... you know what I mean,' Leith persisted. She knew there was a strong physical attraction between herself and Mace Benedict, and from her own point of view she rather felt it might even go beyond that, given a chance, but she couldn't see Mace putting attractiveness ahead of his principles, and he certainly made no bones about his feelings against hobby farmers who wasted good farmland.

'Yes, I know what you mean,' Helen continued. 'But what I don't know is why you insist on classing yourself as being among the dreaded landwasters. You've only been here a short time; you've never pretended to be anything you're not, and certainly you've got some feeling for your property or you wouldn't be here in the first place. I'd think it's a bit premature to be making judgments, and from what I know of Mace Benedict, he'd think so too. Maybe he just likes you. Isn't that enough?'

Enough? If he'd never kissed her, never showed her how responsive she could be ... well, maybe. But now it could never be quite enough, although Leith certainly wasn't going to admit that ... not to anyone. And yet ... it would have to be enough, she thought. Certainly there could be no expectation on her part that anything more might be forthcoming; not with somebody like Madeline involved.

'Yes ... well, perhaps I'm just suspicious by nature,' she finally replied, hoping to close the subject once and for all.

Helen, thankfully, took the hint, and during the rest of her visit they discussed things of rather less consequence than Mace Benedict and his past, present or future attitudes towards Leith.

During the next few weeks, Leith spent a portion of each day working specifically towards training Snap, although she found building a good relationship with the pup far easier than trying to make sense out of the various books on sheepdog training she could get from the library.

And during that time she had occasion quite often to bless the day Mace found her the dog. Snap, once accustomed to Leith and the yard which they shared, almost immediately began to show up the watchdog aspects of her heritage. Not a vehicle so much as slowed outside the house without drawing a warning growl and bark from the small dog, and without Leith there to advise her, Snap would let no one at all through the gate.

It was, Leith decided, rather pleasant. The pup was good with her poultry despite a tendency to try and round up the ducks at feeding time, and best of all, showed no inclination whatsoever to stray. Where Leith went, the dog followed, never more than a few feet away. And that was a great relief, especially when one weekend newspaper featured quite an article on roaming dogs and the havoc they created among flocks of sheep and goats.

Leith's own lambs seemed to be considered by the pup to be of special significance. She didn't exactly try to herd them, but whenever Leith stood and watched them, staring across the fence and wondering how she had ever progressed from potter to shepherd, the dog would stand and stare at the sheep with even greater intensity, as if trying to make the recalcitrant animals pay attention to their mistress.

But Leith had no opportunity to thank Mace Benedict in person. Although she rather expected a visit, this expectation dwindled as day after day passed with only her work to keep her occupied. There were no visitors, not even so much as a telephone call.

On one of her sales trips, she acquired a rooster, a brilliantly coloured, strutting little bantam rooster that rode home in a sack and within minutes of his arrival had taken a serious peck at Snap and made his intentions known to the three inherited hens in no uncertain fashion.

Even more important, he immediately took charge of the three hens and insisted on them roosting each night in the chicken coop, which allowed Leith some control over the location of their nests and the increased flow of eggs that followed close on his arrival.

Encouraged by this small success, she went out the next weekend and bought a drake to service her three ducks. He was a splendid fellow, with russet breast and shining green head, and the only dissatisfaction she found with that arrangement was the breeder's comment that if he mated with her Muscovy duck, the resulting ducklings would be infertile themselves.

'But great for the table,' he'd said, which made a lot of sense in theory but somewhat less in practice. Somehow Leith didn't see herself lopping the heads off an entire clutch of ducklings, but when the time came, as surely it would, in time, she would have to force herself.

Like the bantam, the drake took virtually no time to establish his chauvinistic superiority, and Leith found the presence of both quite an aesthetic improvement to the property. The colourful plumage of the male birds, she thought, might have justified their existence even without their more serious function on the farm.

Her own work, too, seemed enhanced by these small barnyard triumphs. Leith found her fingers strengthened by the hard work, her eyes keener, her sense of symmetry and form somehow improved. She was working more quickly, more surely, and since she could now devote most of each day to her pottery, the quantity increased along with the quality.

Another two weeks, she reckoned, and the mud bricks would be properly cured so that she could start

on her wood-fired kiln. Already she had several pieces
specially set aside for that first firing.

She invited George and Helen up for dinner one
evening, and was thrilled when she was complimented
on the condition of her growing lambs. Somehow it was
more important, more satisfying, than George's open
compliments about her cooking.

'I'd move them into that other paddock fairly soon,
though,' he said. 'They've got the grass down fairly well
where they are, and the change will keep the other from
getting too high. Sheep don't fancy long grass, if they've
a choice, and changing them back and forth will help
keep down the parasite problems.'

Leith listened, and next morning she and Snap
managed to shift the animals without a hint of
difficulty, the pup working as well as might be expected
for her age and the sheep, under the direction of Mace's
matron ewes, behaving with astonishing docility. They
moved in on the new grass with every sign of pleasure,
leaving Leith flushed with pleasure at the success of the
exercise.

In another month, she thought, or perhaps only in
three weeks, she would move them again, this time into
the house paddock, where the grass seemed to grow
even as she watched it. And that was something of a
problem, or certainly would be in another couple of
months when the drying summer winds came.

The grass elsewhere on the property also was
growing, and growing more rapidly than Leith could
ever have imagined. George had volunteered to cut one
paddock for hay when he did his own, but the steepness
of the two largest paddocks would prohibit that
alternative, at least with the small tractor and
equipment he had access to, he'd said.

If only the fences were better, she could rent the land
for agistment. Throughout Tasmania, growing problems
of drought were causing farmers serious concern, but
Leith's position on the shoulder of the mountain meant
she caught virtually every drop of rain that was
available in her district. There was great difference

between the height and quality of her grazing and that even only a few miles away, in the valley.

If only she could somehow afford to fix the fences, she thought. If only she could afford to do a lot of things, but she couldn't and that was that. Except that it was wasteful, and much as she hated to accept that fact, because it meant renewed thoughts of Mace Benedict and his comments, Leith had to accept it. The problem was what to do about it, and the solution arrived two days later from a most unexpected source.

The man who called at the door, braving Snap's toothsome warnings, was young, no more than in his early twenties. And Leith had to smile to herself at his tongue-tied embarrassment as he ducked his head and handed her a note. Then she read the note and her smile disappeared.

'Leith. This will introduce Anson Jones, who's going to fix up your main paddock fences in return for being able to run some sheep on your place. He's desperate for the grass, and I knew you wouldn't object to helping out a neighbour.'

The note was signed, of course, 'Mace Benedict', but it wasn't the signature that upset Leith so much as the high-handed, autocratic manner. Damn him, she thought. He could have 'phoned, or stopped by, or, or *something*! At the very least he could have asked. What possible right did he think he had to arbitrarily decide such a thing?

But she couldn't take it out on the shy young man who seemed poised for instant flight. It certainly wasn't his fault. Leith caught her breath quickly, then spoke equally quickly to cover up the signs of raging temper inside her.

She invited the young man to have coffee before he got started, wasn't in the least surprised at his refusal, and spent the next hour showing him the extent of the fencing, the worst portions as she knew them, and trying desperately to winkle some information from him about how this arrangement had come about. But it was like talking to one of the stumps, or to a fence post.

Young Anson Jones was so overcome with shyness that it was all she could do to get him to speak at all.

He'd arrived in a battered old utility loaded with wire and steel posts and all the paraphernalia required for the job at hand, so Leith finally decided it was best to just get out of his way and let him get on with it, which he did with obvious relief at her decision.

But her own work plans were blown sky-high by the unexpected development; she was frothing inside with indignation at Mace Benedict and his high-handed ways, and her anger made any attempt at creative pottery impossible. Finally, in desperation for someone to talk to, someone she could pour out her anger to, she drove down to Helen's and demanded coffee and a responsive ear.

She got the coffee. 'It seems like a splendid suggestion to me,' the older woman said after listening to Leith. 'Young Jones is a good lad, if a bit slow up top. And he would need the grass; he's got a fair mob of wethers on his bush runs and his own grazing will be gone by now.'

'I don't dispute that he needs the grass, and he's welcome to it,' Leith raged. 'What bothers me is the damned, autocratic, male chauvinist fashion in which it's all been arranged. I mean ... couldn't somebody have at least *asked* me? Is that too much to expect, even from the likes of Mace Benedict?'

'No sense asking me,' Helen shrugged. And her entire attitude made it clear that she thought Leith was making far too much of the issue. After all, it had solved two problems for two people, which was the purpose of the exercise, so why get all upset?

'No, you're right,' Leith agreed with a sigh. 'It's Mace Benedict I should be asking, and never fear, I intend to do just that!'

But the problem, she found, wasn't in asking Mace Benedict; it was in finding him. He wasn't at home, wasn't at his office in the city—not that she had really expected to find him there—and nobody had any idea, it seemed, just where he might be located.

Not even his mother, although Fiona Benedict clearly knew about his arrangement on Leith's behalf with Anson Jones.

'I'm so pleased you agreed to help out,' Fiona said after being assured that yes, Anson Jones was even now busy repairing the fences, but Leith didn't know exactly when he'd be bringing up his mob of sheep.

'Of course, I knew you'd help, especially since it's such an ideal arrangement for you both. Anson is very good at fencing, too, so you can be assured of a first-class job.'

'I really wasn't worried about that,' Leith said. 'It just seems ... well ... isn't it going to be awfully expensive?'

'Not at all. Mace told me you had a large quantity of posts and droppers about the place, and the original wire should be all right,' Mrs Benedict assured her. 'Anson could surely spare a couple of days to do the work, so in the end you'll both benefit tremendously. The only problem ... well ... I don't quite know how to ask this, Leith, but Mace was ... reasonably diplomatic when he approached you about this, I suppose?'

Leith gurgled with laughter; she couldn't help it. And then she had to smother the laugh and with it the tart reply that automatically came to mind. It wouldn't do to upset Mrs Benedict; it wasn't her fault, after all.

'Oh yes, he was totally diplomatic,' Leith finally managed to say, gritting her teeth around the lie and doubling in her mind the price Mace would pay for deceiving both she and his mother. The nerve!

After her conversation with Fiona, she made up some coffee and walked down to the bottom paddock with a thermos full for Anson Jones, who would likely need it, she thought, after the work he'd been up to.

And if it didn't make him too nervous, perhaps she would watch for a bit and try to learn something of the task herself. As Leith strolled towards the gate dividing her paddocks, she began to admit that the arrangement *was* extremely beneficial—if only Mace had used some of the diplomacy his mother so mistakenly credited to him.

Then she crested the ridge and looked down to see not one man, but two, busy repairing the sagging fence at the paddock bottom.

Two men, and, yes ... two vehicles. The other man must have driven in while Leith was down at Helen's, she thought, and then as recognition dawned, her vision blurred in sheets of fury. Mace Benedict! Yes, it was; no mistaking that lean, muscular figure, the shock of inky hair, the casual wave of recognition as he noted her approach.

Leith was trembling by the time she completed the trek to where both men had paused momentarily in their labours. Her eyes flashed venom at Mace, even as she flashed an equally warm smile for his companion and proferred the thermos of coffee.

'I thought you might be ready for this,' she said calmly, waving aside Anson's stammered thanks. Then she turned so that the younger man couldn't see the glare she unleashed as she spoke in the same calm voice to Mace Benedict.

'Well, if I'd known you were going to be here, I'd have brought a second cup,' she said. 'But then I hardly expected to see you ... here.'

'Don't worry about it,' was the equally calm reply, but Mace's black eyes laughed at her, showing that he saw and understood the look of fury. 'I'm not real partial to arsenic with my coffee anyway.'

And he had the gall to laugh out loud at her frown and half-hidden shrug towards their companion. Leith could have screamed, except she knew it wouldn't accomplish anything. How could this arrogant man's mother even *think* of him being diplomatic?

'Actually, I'd planned to get here ahead of Anson,' Mace was saying, totally ignoring the furious glare she was giving him. 'But I thought I might get caught up— which, in fact, I did—so I gave him that note just in case. Just as well I did, from the look of it.'

Leith took a firm grip on her temper ... and her

tongue. 'So I see,' she replied. 'You do tend to think of everything, don't you, *Mister* Benedict? Although of course it never seemed to occur to you to think that I might have already made my own arrangements, or even that I might just simply object to your little proposal?'

His shrug was non-committal; not so his reply. 'I certainly didn't think you'd object to such an obviously beneficial arrangement,' he said. 'And as for other arrangements, well, perhaps you've got a point there. Although I really would have expected I'd have heard about it if you had.'

'Oh you would, would you?' Leith's voice rose as the anger began to slip its leash. And this time it was Mace who shot a sideways glance to where Anson Jones was drinking his coffee and apparently paying no attention to their argument.

As Leith's eyes began to flash warning signs, Snap caught the scent of anger and began to charge about beneath Leith's feet, brown eyes pleading for explanation and her pink tongue bared in a series of shrill yips.

'If you were just a bit bigger I'd let you eat him,' Leith muttered, bending to calm the excited dog. 'But at your age you'd likely only get indigestion from such an arrogant, pompous, know-it-all.'

Suddenly she knew she couldn't stay any longer, not without making a scene even slow-witted Anson couldn't miss. Teeth clenched around her words, she grated, 'I can't take any more of this. Please have him drop off the thermos when he leaves.'

And without waiting for a reply from Mace Benedict, damn his arrogant soul anyway, she strode away back up the hill, struggling to contain tears of frustration and anger.

Beneath her feet, yelping shrill little barks of anxiety, Snap scampered back and forth, occasionally leaping up to nip at Leith's sleeves and trouser cuffs.

Leith half expected Mace to try and stop her going, or perhaps to follow and continue the argument, but she wasn't overly surprised when he did not. As she reached the crest of the ridge, her ears picked up the sounds of the men resuming them work, and she breathed a sigh of relief as she passed quickly out of their sight.

But once back at the house, Leith found herself totally at a loss for what to do next. Her every instinct told her that she hadn't seen the last of Mace Benedict for that day; he was sure to stop in before leaving the property.

And what was she to say? Nothing in his attitude had in any way soothed her temper. He not only hadn't apologised for trying to totally organise her life, but he seemed—like everyone else in the district—to feel it was the logical thing to have done.

'But it wasn't!' Leith moaned the denial, nearly as angry with herself as with Mace. Certainly his decision had created a situation from which she would benefit, and even more certainly she knew she'd never have refused exactly the same arrangement had Anson Jones come and asked himself, or if George or Helen had asked. But to have it thrust upon her without consultation, without even so much as the courtesy of a request—no! That, she decided, was too much altogether.

Her mind turned to Mace Benedict as she'd seen him last, dark hair curled on his brow with the perspiration of his labours, workshirt half open to the waist as he leaned on the heavy fencing crowbar. And that damned, infectious, defiant grin, a grin that could melt stone, much less her own susceptibility.

Leith prowled the house, polishing, dusting, knowing she was only killing time, only trying to free her mind and doing an extremely poor job of both that and the house-cleaning. She badly wanted to return to the bottom paddock, to have it out with Mace Benedict once and for all. But she couldn't, not without putting an intolerable burden on poor Anson Jones. And yet . . . she couldn't not! This type of thing simply couldn't be allowed to continue, or the next thing she knew he'd be trying to take over the rest of her life.

The rest of the afternoon was torture. She couldn't settle, yet she could no more work than fly to the moon. Her entire mind was fixed on the confrontation she knew must come, the confrontation she would force all by herself, if necessary.

It was nearly dark when the two men finished, and they came to the house together. And as Leith might have anticipated, Mace did the talking, made the arrangements, in a fashion which gave her little room to manoeuvre.

'Anson reckons he can be done by tomorrow afternoon sometime, then bring up the sheep the next morning if that's okay with you,' he said, neither servile nor arrogant in his manner of asking.

'Yes, I suppose so,' she replied, more aware of Anson Jones' rather sheepish attitude than of Mace Benedict's direct appraisal. Since the decisions all seemed to have been made, it would only be childish to start disagreeing at this stage.

'We've had to use a fair number of your posts and droppers, I'm afraid,' Mace continued. 'But Anson reckons he'll be able to cut you a bunch to replace them . . .'

'Oh, for goodness' sake,' Leith interrupted. 'Why shouldn't you have used them? It's my fence, after all. Tell him he's welcome to use them all, if it'll make it any easier, and certainly he doesn't have to worry about replacing them. I'd only end up using them for firewood or something anyway.'

She could feel her control slipping, but if the younger man noticed he was too polite to show it. Mace merely looked at her with a slightly bemused expression for a moment, then turned to his companion.

'She's only having you on, mate,' he said with a wry grin. 'But she's right about the posts. By the time we're finished tomorrow she shouldn't need any more before next spring anyhow. You go off now and tend to your chores at home, and I'll see you back here bright and early.'

The comments brought him a wide grin, then Anson

bobbed his head to Leith and trotted off to his truck, giving Snap a caress as he passed. A moment later he was gone in a cloud of blue smoke, leaving Leith to face Mace Benedict without any support at all.

She looked up, finally, to meet a glance that was totally unreadable. His black eyes seemed fathomless, like inky pools that gave no indication of what he was thinking, what he would say. And suddenly her own well-rehearsed assault seemed to swell in her mouth, refusing to step out into the cloud of tension between them.

'Well,' he said, and then paused. Leith said nothing. She could only stare at him, feeling like some helpless animal being mesmerised by a predator. Mace stood there, the epitome of masculine strength and power, and she found herself almost cowering despite the intellectual wish to strike out, to scream and rail at him, to demand his apologies, force some sort of reaction from him.

'Well,' he said again, 'if you're going to get stuck into me, I wish you'd hurry up and get it over with. You'll make a damned poor dinner companion if you're planning on staying angry forever.'

Leith stared at him, trying to make sense out of his words. Dinner companion? What did he expect now— that she'd feed him as well? But then he was speaking again, and she had to close off her own thoughts in order to listen.

'Being angry really doesn't suit you,' he said. 'It takes all the softness out of your eyes. Usually they're just like soft grey velvet, and I think I rather prefer that to the way they are now.' And he raised one sooty eyebrow, a slow smile quirking about his lips.

'Nothing to say? Or is it all so drastic you're afraid to let such language pass your lips? Go ahead and swear if you like; even my mother does, occasionally.'

'Your mother,' Leith finally growled through gritted teeth, 'should have drowned you at birth.'

'Or at the very least given me a hiding once a week just to keep me in line?' he asked. And that damnable grin was still there; he was really enjoying himself, Leith thought, which only served to fuel the fires of her growing anger.

'Why don't you just please leave?' she asked. 'I really don't think we have a single thing to talk about, now that the ... arrangements ... have been made.'

'And without even asking you. That's what you're all shirty about, isn't it?' Mace replied without bothering to recognise her demands.

'Well shouldn't I be?' she fairly screeched. 'My God, but you're an arrogant, insensitive man! You run around making deals that will affect my property for months to come and you expect me to just sit here and accept that blindly, without question? Yes, Mr Benedict; anything you say, Mr Benedict; of course, Mr Benedict; oh, how clever of you, Mr Benedict?'

Leith shivered, feeling the cold icicle of pure rage stiffening her spine. 'Well I say this: Go to hell, Mr Benedict! Do not pass Go; do not collect $200; just GO ... TO ... HELL!'

And then she stopped. She could feel her lips trembling, feel the trembling run through her body, and she knew if she said another word she would very likely burst into tears and destroy the entire effect of her outburst.

'You're probably right, of course. I should have asked you,' he said then, his voice surprisingly soft, yet incisive enough to cut through the mental blocks she was busily erecting. Leith tried to close her ears, to shut out the sound of that deceptively soothing voice, but it was no use. 'I did try to 'phone,' he continued, 'but you must have been outside or something. And then ... well ... I was pretty busy and I couldn't see tying Anson up any longer than necessary, especially as I honestly did expect to get here in time to discuss it with you before he actually arrived.'

'I don't care!' Leith cried, but she knew she was lying. She did care; she did want some sort of explanation, however flimsy.

'Of course you care; you wouldn't be so angry,

otherwise,' he said. 'And I care too, because the object of the exercise wasn't to upset you, it was to be helpful. I didn't set out to make you angry.'

'You do not care,' Leith snarled. 'It never even occurred to you that I might expect to be consulted. Or even that I should be, because as far as you're concerned I'm just a hobby farmer and I wouldn't know if it was a good idea or not anyway, so why bother to ask. Oh, no . . . your way was so much easier, wasn't it?'

The outburst thrust new life into her frozen limbs. She lunged at him, pummelling with her fists against the hard muscles of his chest, kicking out at him. But she might have been assaulting a tree, or one of the immovable fence posts he'd been erecting all the day.

Mace took it for a moment, then reached out and clasped her shoulders, his fingers firm as iron clamps, yet somehow gentle, not bruising her, not grating into her flesh, merely holding her immobile. And then, drawing her against him, pulling her softness against the warm firmness of his body.

'Oh, Leith,' he muttered harshly, lips only an inch from her ear. 'Can't I even apologise without a fight?'

She wanted to answer, tried to answer, but it was too late. His lips were firm on her own, forcing back the words, burning away her anger, her frustration, burning with a strange, cool, fire to which her body had no defence.

Leith found her mouth moulding to his, her body not fighting the shape of his embrace, but yielding to it, allow his hands to bring her close against him, so that his bodily warmth flowed between them in a river of slowly-rising turbulence.

There was a tiny instant, when his hands released her shoulders to move slowly down her body, fingers exploring the contours of her back, that Leith could have resisted, should have reared back out of range. But she was held by his mouth, captured by the sweetness of his breath, the very taste of him.

Then her own moan of acquiescence was wordless,

though no less a surrender for that. Her hands lifted to pull his head down, crushing his lips against hers with greater force than he had exerted.

The fingers at her waist co-operated, pulling them closer together, melding the softness of breast with the muscular hardness of male chest, the different textures of hip and thigh. Leith's fingers explored the powerful neck muscles, the softer but even more powerful muscles of his shoulders and back.

She was breathless from his kisses, yet so exhilarated that she felt no need to breathe; she was floating, held in his arms as lightly as if she were weightless.

And then her feet were firmly on the ground, his voice harsh in her ears as he growled, 'Snap! Damn it, dog, cut that out, you bloody ungrateful little horror.'

Leith took an instant to recover her composure, then looked down to see her dog, puppy teeth clashing like castanets when they weren't meeting in Mace Benedict's ankle.

'Ouch! I said stop, damn it!' A huge hand plunged down to lift the enraged puppy by the scruff of her neck, then one forefinger shook itself in admonishment as he scolded the animal.

'Nooooooo biting. Nooooo. None! You're a baaaad dog. Now leave it.'

Leith couldn't help it. She broke right up, dissolving in helpless laughter at the angry expression on Mace's features and the determined, remorseless clatter of the puppy's jaws as it squirmed to get a grip on the shaking finger, the hand at its ruff, anything biteable within range.

'I . . . I think she doesn't like you,' Leith stammered, still shaking with laughter. Reaching out, she took the pup from Mace's hand and quietly began assuring Snap that she wasn't being assaulted, that it was all right. And when she released the pup, who immediately made to resume the attack, a distinct 'No!' was sufficient to stop Snap.

'And after all I've done for you,' Mace muttered at the dog. 'Here I've found you the best of homes, and how do you repay me? I should have let you be shot; it's just what you deserve.'

And for just that instant, he sounded so serious that Leith caught her breath, then released it just as quickly as he bent to stroke the now-compliant puppy. 'That's better,' he murmured as a pink tongue emerged to lick at his hand, then he straightened up to smile at Leith.

'Well, she's going to prove mightily useful for one thing, anyway,' he said. 'Nobody's likely to lay a hand on you with this dog around, whether you want them to or not.'

'And just as well,' Leith responded vehemently, still shaken from the tremendous reaction his kisses had stirred within her.

'Yes, probably it is,' Mace agreed. 'Now what say you go and change, because what you're wearing is hardly suitable for going out to dinner.'

'No!' The refusal popped into her mouth without conscious thought. But once said, she found it the right reply, for her, for this moment. She wanted time to sort out her feelings, to try and gain a grip on her disrupted emotions; she wouldn't get that by dining with the very cause of the problem.

'Yes!' His attitude was equally adamant, even when softened by the warmth of the smile that accompanied it. 'It's part of the apology, and you can't take half without the rest.'

'Who said I'd accepted any part of it?' she retorted, then wished she could bite her tongue.

'Your lips said so, and your body did too,' he replied softly, but with a gleam in his eyes she couldn't miss. 'Or should we resume the conversation just to make you a bit more sure?'

'I doubt if your ankles could stand the strain,' Leith replied, trying to keep her voice light, keep the tremor hidden from the man who so easily created it within her.

'There's a perfectly good kennel in which to solve that particular problem,' Mace said, masking the seriousness of his tone with an even broader grin. 'Or we could just shift into the house and leave Miss Toothsome out here.'

'I think not,' Leith replied soberly. 'In fact, I think I shall take the dog in the house, and you can go on with whatever you've planned for this evening—without me!'

'Oh, no. It wouldn't be the same without you,' Mace grinned. 'Now stop being difficult and go get changed. I'll be back to pick you up in an hour.'

And before Leith could reply, he was out the gate and already climbing into his vehicle. 'I am not coming with you,' she shouted at his retreating figure, but he either didn't hear her or ignored the last-word gesture.

'Well I'm not,' she muttered to herself as she watched the vehicle drive away. 'Damned, arrogant so-and-so.' The words issued through lips puffy and bruised from his kisses, and it was the kisses she relived, not the fight she'd had before them.

Leith spent the following hour in a dither of haphazard activity—none of it involving anything like getting ready to accompany Mace for dinner. She fed the dog, gave it half an hour's training, and then tried to force herself to read, although she knew she was wasting her time trying to concentrate on fiction when the factual part of her life was getting so out of hand as to be frightening.

How could she possibly react so strongly to this one man's kisses? She'd been kissed before, but never with such devastating effect. And she'd found herself at loggerheads with various men before, too, yet never had any of them been so able to shift her from rage to passion and back again with what seemed in retrospect to be sheer, competent skill.

The hour passed, and when Mace hadn't turned up, she smiled to herself and tried to be pleased that he *had* listened to her final words. 'Although why he should, I can't imagine; he's never listened to anything else I've said,' she muttered aloud, annoyed that she wasn't really pleased, but was in fact disappointed.

Until he did arrive, no more than five minutes later. Then she watched him stroll towards the gate, white shirt gleaming against the dark of his suit.

She flung open the door at his knock, mouth half-open to utter a stern rebuff, but was caught short when he spoke first.

'Well, I certainly didn't expect you to go to all that trouble,' he said, one eyebrow raised in sardonic comment. 'It's only dinner, you know, not an audience with the Queen.'

'It is not! Damn you, I said when you left that I wouldn't be coming. Don't you listen?'

He shrugged, a maddening, supercilious gesture. 'Must have misunderstood,' he said quietly. 'Ah well, I suppose it won't be the worst disappointment Mum's had to endure in her life. Are you going to 'phone and make your apologies, or does that fall on my shoulders?'

'You . . . your mother?' Leith couldn't conceal the gasp of astonishment and—now—of confusion. What to do? She couldn't possibly be so rude to Mace's mother, whom she quite liked, and yet . . .

'I'll dial for you, if you like.'

The bastard! He knew . . . he *knew* the position he was putting her in, and damn his soul, he was enjoying it, too. Leith fairly fumed with outrage at the complacent scheming to which she was being subjected.

'Oh . . . you . . . just give me five minutes,' she cried, and fled to her bedroom, leaving him standing at the door. As she flung clothing helter-skelter, her befuddled mind racing with the need for decisions, she was also cursing Mace Benedict for a scheming, rotten sod, and doing it out loud. If he heard, too bad!

When she emerged from the bedroom *en route* to the shower, he was sitting silently at her kitchen table, and he merely glanced up with a sardonic smirk at her towel-wrapped figure as it passed. Leith slammed the door, hoping against hope it would burst his ear-drums, but knowing it wouldn't so much as still his tongue. Nor did it!

'Yes, that's much better,' he murmured as she was forced to pass him again in order to reach her bedroom and her clothes. 'Mum mightn't be too impressed, but I certainly am.'

'Oh . . . shut up!' she snapped, flinging the door shut behind her. But once in the bedroom she found herself choosing her clothing with rather more care than she would have liked to admit. Fair enough for Fiona Benedict, but she also couldn't ignore the fact that Mace had never seen her in anything but jeans and work shirts. And a towel, she thought irreverently, then tried vainly to dismiss that thought and the tingle it brought to her skin.

She dithered briefly, then settled on her best outfit, a pearl-grey evening suit that almost exactly matched her eyes. Coupled with a white frilled shirt and black coral necklace and ear-rings, it blended style and sophistication without being gaudy, and Leith knew it suited her very well indeed.

As she worked on her tights, she wished half-heartedly she'd not been quite so stubborn in the first place. Then she'd at least have had time to wash her hair, though it didn't really need it, and perhaps even do a major repair job on her nails, which did need it . . . badly.

Overall, the transformation took rather more than five minutes, but less than fifteen, Leith thought with pride as she dabbed on some perfume and strode confidently through to where Mace still sat waiting in the kitchen.

'I've put the dog in her run,' he said without looking up, then did raise his head, and Leith stirred at the undisguised look of pleasure she saw revealed in his eyes.

'My very word,' he said slowly, voice almost in a whisper. And rose to bow to her in almost courtly fashion. 'It's a good thing you didn't take the full hour; I'd have been forced to take you somewhere far more splendid than just home for dinner with Mum.'

'If it were anywhere else, I wouldn't be going, remember?' she chided lightly, then smiled to show she wasn't serious. Now. The touch of his glance was a

caress all in its own, and she revelled unshamedly in a
Mace Benedict caress that had at least some modicum
of safety for her acceptance of it.

The drive to the Benedict homestead was conducted
in relative silence. Mace steered the luxurious
Mercedes—a distinct change from his workaday
vehicle—down the mountain with an almost casual
aptitude while Leith leaned back against the luxurious
seats and listened to the soft music emerging from the
stereo cassette deck.

Once on the bitumen, the huge car hummed along
in an almost ghostly silence, and still Mace seemed to
find no great need for conversation, although Leith
might have welcomed some to try and allay the
sudden nervousness. It was one thing, she discovered,
coping with this man when both of them were in
work clothing and shared some common ground, but
now, dressed up, and once they reached his home . . .
his own ground . . .

There was no need for her nervousness. Fiona
Benedict greeted her warmly, even complimenting her
on her dress in a fashion so totally genuine that Leith
immediately felt more at ease.

Mace produced pre-dinner drinks for all of them, and
they settled into an easy, relaxed conversation that
had—thankfully—nothing to do with fencing or lost
sheep or Leith's inexperience at country living. It also
gave Leith her first real chance to observe Mace
Benedict at a time when she, herself, wasn't at some
sort of disadvantage, and she found that here, in his
own home, he was as gracious and charming a host as
she might have imagined.

It was clear that he enjoyed a warm and loving
relationship with his mother, and that the authori-
tarianism Leith seemed to arouse in him wasn't a
part of that relationship.

Leith was just settling down, starting to really relax,
when a rushing crunch of gravel outside announced a
new arrival. But the unexpected part was that neither
Mace nor his mother seemed at all surprised when

Madeline DeMers appeared at the door. Had she been expected? Leith didn't know, although it certainly hadn't been mentioned. Her only slight satisfaction was that Madeline seemed at least equally astonished to find Leith in the Benedict house!

CHAPTER SIX

'WELL, this is a surprise,' Madeline said almost immediately upon entering the room. And her cold eyes, glittering with a hostility that belied the apparent warmth of her smile, told Leith that it wasn't a pleasant surprise.

The tall, dark-haired woman *must* have been invited to dinner, Leith thought. She was dressed in a very revealing, very flattering and obviously *very* expensive outfit of dark green velvet that flowed around her curvaceous figure. It made Leith's own outfit look almost dowdy by comparison.

'You didn't tell me there'd be company for dinner,' Madeline continued, turning upon Fiona Benedict in mock seriousness. 'I shouldn't have worn this old thing if I'd known; I thought it was to be just . . . family.'

And the way she said it, deliberately establishing Leith as the outsider, set the tone of her entire conversation throughout the evening that followed. Madeline positively dominated the conversation, linking herself to Mace in a continuous barrage of talk in which Leith had no knowledge and could contribute nothing. It was all about people she didn't know and incidents in a shared past where she had no place.

Only Fiona Benedict made any obvious attempt to keep Leith involved, but her efforts to make Leith feel welcome were invariably put down as quickly as they arose. Mace didn't seem to notice how Madeline dominated both the conversation and his mother; he, himself, said little during the excellent dinner of roast spring lamb and all the usual trimmings.

As if encouraged by her initial successes, Madeline began after dinner to slant the talk more Leith's way, posing questions in such a way as to provoke clumsy or—at best—incriminating answers.

'It certainly must have been difficult for you to make such a decision about leaving Sydney for Tasmania,' she began. 'I mean, surely you had a boyfriend or two who would have objected? Or didn't their opinions matter to you?'

Leith almost chuckled at the blatancy of it. Fortified by the excellent meal, the wine with dinner and the warm glow of first-rate brandy afterwards, she found the question almost expected. Madeline was nothing more, she thought, than a female version of Brian— scheming, calculating, but threatening only if she, herself, allowed it.

Brian, too, had used words as weapons, twisting them to suit his own purposes, creating from words a form of emotional blackmail, an ability to create guilt where none had existed.

'It was a very easy decision, really,' she replied, almost as if the question itself held no real importance. And she smiled sweetly at her interrogator. Madeline, Leith had decided, would have to really push things, if upsetting Leith was her objective.

But it wasn't Madeline who spoke up next; to Leith's great surprise it was Mace—and he appeared to be taking her side.

'Leith doesn't need a lot of help in making her decisions,' he said, rather drily, she thought. 'It's one of the perks of being a truly liberated woman.' The final words emerged, Leith thought, as if they made a bad taste in his mouth. Could he really object that strongly to her attempts at independence? Or was it just that he still believed her incapable of managing on her own?

Madeline, too, must have caught the nuance. And revelled in it. 'You make it sound like some horrid disease, Mace,' she said in a perfectly smarmy voice, almost gloating as she fixed dark eyes on Leith to catch her reaction. 'Perhaps being liberated suits Leith; after all, she has plenty of opportunity to practise it, buried back in the bush as she is.'

The innuendo was hardly subtle, and the last thing Madeline expected, obviously, was for Leith to pick up the insinuation and carry it even further. Which is exactly what she did, and quite deliberately.

'There's a great deal to be said for such privacy,' Leith replied with a slow grin at Madeline's flash of astonishment at such agreement. 'I quite enjoy the opportunities it affords.'

'Well I certainly couldn't imagine such a thing for myself,' was the reply. 'Practically living like a hermit, I'd call it. Or is it,' and she paused slightly with a speculative gleam in her eye that warned Leith, 'part of the artistic syndrome? Like starving in garrets or some such thing?'

'Hardly that,' Leith replied, 'although I suppose I must admit I find the privacy conducive to getting plenty of . work done. Certainly there aren't the interruptions, generally, that one might find living in the city. Nor the distractions.'

She paused herself then, debating momentarily whether to continue and risk Mace's disagreement or wisely shut her mouth and. let Madeline carry the conversation. No, she'd set the pace herself, Leith decided. And hopefully she might change the tone of the conversation sufficiently to give her a chance to extricate herself entirely from it by a reasonably timely suggestion about going home.

'I gather that you wouldn't fancy such a life-style at all?' she asked Madeline, already knowing the answer but wanting to hear the other woman's version, in her own words.

'Lord no!' was the emphatic reply. 'Not that I mind life in the country when there's reasonable access to the amenities,' and her eyes roved around the oppulent furnishings of the room where they sat, 'but to hibernate back in the bush as you're doing, well, I think I'd have to be in a situation where I had something to hide.'

'Maybe Leith fancies herself as a modern-day bushranger,' Mace said, flashing both girls a rather indulgent grin. 'There's certainly the precedent for it up where she lives.'

And he grinned mischievously at the curious glances his comment had aroused. 'Really, possum, I'd have expected *you* at least to know your local history better than that,' he said then. 'Leith has some excuse, I suppose, but you certainly haven't.'

Both girls still looked bemused, although it was obvious Mrs Benedict knew what her son was talking about, so he explained.

'Martin Cash, one of Tasmania's most famous bushrangers . . . I can tell you that much,' he said. 'He and his companions had a stronghold atop "The Dromedary" as it was referred to in those days. It was little more than a pile of logs at the very top of the mountain, but think of the view they would have had.'

Rising lithely to his feet, he strode from the room then without explanation, returning a moment later with a small book in his hands.

'Martin Cash: His personal narrative as a bushranger in Van Diemen's Land,' he read from the cover. Then turned open the book. 'Yes, I thought it was about then. 1843–44. And I recall he had friends living at Cobb's Hill, which is well down the mountain and south of your place, Leith, although I wouldn't be surprised if your property saw a bit of him on his travels as well.'

'Surely it wouldn't be as old as all that,' Leith replied, but she knew even as she spoke that it might well be. The enormous pines in the house paddock said different; they might well have been tiny seedlings or even young adults when Martin Cash and his men rode by.

'Just as I said,' Madeline broke in spitefully. 'A good place for somebody with something to hide. What are you hiding, Leith? Or . . . hiding from, if that's a closer guess?'

'You'd hardly expect me to tell, surely,' Leith replied almost absently, her imagination stirred and caught by the brief glimpses of the historic bushranger. 'Far more likely I should skulk the road at night with a brace of pistols and a sabre, shouting "Stand and Deliver!"'

'You'd best take this home with you and read it, before you try any wild stunts like that,' Mace said, rising to hand the book over. 'It was no easy life as a bushranger, if this narrative is true, though I suppose today's gaols are an improvement over the situation that existed at Port Arthur in those days.'

'Ah, but they'd have to catch me first,' Leith cried, waving wildly about with an imaginary sabre. 'And they'd not do it on my own mountain.'

Her thoughts seemed to amuse everyone but Madeline, who insisted—to no avail—on trying to return the conversation to whatever Leith might be hiding, or hiding from, on her mountain. Mace and his mother, however, joined Leith in dreaming up impossible scenarios in which she kidnapped rich graziers, shot the tyres off intruding weekend wood-hawkers' vehicles and created general mayhem in the community.

Madeline was forced, finally, to join in the laughter as the ideas became totally ridiculous, but Leith could see only coldness beneath the laughs from the dark-haired woman, and venom in her every glance. Did she object so much to this small bit of scene-stealing, Leith wondered? Or did she seriously think there was competition in a small, blonde hobby-farmer?

Either way, Leith found the thinly disguised hatred disquieting, and was glad when she could finally call a halt to the evening, pleading an early start next morning. She was even gladder when Mace gently but firmly rejected Madeline's offer to drive Leith home; it would be a much braver bushranger than she to brave the mountain road with Madeline—hating her—behind the wheel.

They drove home in relative silence, Leith having exhausted her own good spirits in the play-acting, and Mace said little until he'd pulled into her driveway to the immediate outburst of Snap's barking.

During the last stages of the drive up the mountain, she'd found herself wondering just exactly how her evening would end. Should she think of inviting Mace in for coffee? Would he come if she did? Not likely, Leith reckoned, with the lure of Madeline drawing him home. Certainly it didn't take much imagination to be sure that Madeline would be staying at the Benedict homestead until Mace returned; the dark-haired girl would be incapable of yielding his attentions that far.

'I'd best not stop long. Tomorrow will be a long, hard day for everybody,' Mace said once the car had stopped. No mention of Madeline, not that Leith had expected any, and now she found herself angered by the other woman's interference in her evening.

'Yes, I'm certain you're expected back just as quick as you can make it,' Leith replied, knowing even as the words passed her lips that she sounded spiteful, perhaps even jealous. No, she thought to herself, not jealous . . . merely spiteful.

'Ah,' he replied softly, dark eyes turning to meet her cold stare. His left arm lifted to drape itself across the seat back behind her, but he made no move to touch Leith, nor did he speak again for a moment.

She sat immobile, also saying nothing, wondering if he would now try to kiss her, what she might do if he did. Only he didn't.

'Still trying to read something new into my every word, eh?' he said softly, and it was more a statement than an accusation, demanding no real answer.

Leith was barely conscious of the words, but was instead almost hypnotised by the intensity of the dark eyes boring into her own. She felt almost breathless, her heart racing, the pulse in her throat like a hammer against the fragile skin.

'Well, let me tell you something, dear Leith . . . not that I expect you to believe it,' Mace drawled softly. 'But I come and go as I please, without being subject much to anybody's expectations. I'm a big boy now, just in case you hadn't noticed, and I make my own decisions.'

'I . . . don't recall saying differently,' Leith replied, her anger now partially submerged in her overall awareness of this man, of his vital masculinity.

'Well then your recollections are as whimsical as the rest of you,' he growled. 'All that femininity hiding behind a flimsy little shield of so-called independence. And it really is flimsy; you couldn't even manage to hide the bit of green-eyed jealousy, even though I'm sure you wouldn't admit that it was jealousy, not even to yourself.'

'I can't imagine why I should admit to something that's only a figment of your rather chauvinistic imagination,' Leith retorted. And wished he didn't always make her lie.

'My imagination? Or your own?' he chuckled. 'Although I suppose it can't hurt to admit that it wasn't me who planned that rather ... unusual dinner grouping tonight. You can blame my match-making mother for that, dear Leith. She has just the kind of mind that would enjoy seating me between two such contrastingly beautiful women, just to watch the sparks fly.'

'Well then she must have been disappointed,' Leith replied almost sulkily. 'Unless of course her imagination is as ridiculous as your own, which I rather doubt.'

'My, aren't we prickly?' he chuckled, this time even more deeply, with more of that smug self-assurance that so easily primed her own temper. 'Maybe I should have let Madeline drive you home; the experience might have frightened some of it out of you.'

'Personally, I don't see why you didn't,' Leith retorted. 'At least I wouldn't have been sitting here in the middle of such a harangue.'

'It must be just me that does these things to you,' he said almost musingly. 'You were certainly less touchy at dinner, despite rather more intense provocation. I can't imagine what Mum was thinking about ... or rather I'd prefer not to think about it. Surprised she didn't invite your realtor boyfriend while she was at it, actually.'

'Considering I don't have any realtor boyfriend, or any other sort for that matter, she was probably just showing more good sense than you ever do,' Leith snapped. 'And now if you don't mind, I think I'll go in now, because I've a long day tomorrow and I'm really not in the mood for inane discussions.'

'No discussion is inane if it enhances understanding,' he replied with a grin. 'Although some of us obviously seem more able to understand than others.'

'Meaning what?' Leith snapped. 'That I'm not understanding, just because I don't agree with your every silly notion?'

'Not even because you won't admit you're just a little bit jealous, although why you should be, I can't imagine,' he replied calmly.

'Well neither can I ... probably because I'm not in the least jealous,' Leith snorted. 'Any ideas you have on that subject, as I've already said, are merely figments of your chauvinistic imagination.'

'Are they?' Mace asked, his voice now strangely soft, alluring. Leith suddenly realised that the hand behind her shoulders now was gentle against the nape of her neck, slowly but inexorably drawing her towards Mace, towards lips that could melt hers with a single touch. She began to pull away, but his fingers were like a velvet vice, holding her easily as he bent his lips to claim her own.

Angry as she was, certain as she was that it was simply a male bid to achieve and maintain dominance, Leith found it impossible to ignore his kisses. When her lips tried to obey her mental direction to remain rigid, unresponding, Mace's mouth seemed somehow able to charm them into accepting his kisses, responding to them in direct defiance of her own wishes. His fingertips at her throat were an exquisite torture, holding her gently as a babe, yet with a total masculine sensuality that made her quiver with reaction.

When his fingertips caressed her breasts, lifting her nipples to turgid, throbbing peaks of pleasure, she moaned in her throat, trying to object but unable to free the words as easily as his manipulative fingers freed her breasts to his lips. Then her moans were not of objection, but of sheer, undiluted pleasure as her lips caressed his hair, the back of his neck, her body afire with sensations she'd never in her life realised could even exist.

'This is madness,' she heard him whisper, felt the breath of him against the throbbing bareness of her breasts as he spoke. Then, 'Come, we'll go inside,' and his arm was beneath her legs, partially lifting her into his arms.

'Nnnnno!' She managed to stammer, wriggling in a last-minute bid to free herself, to stop what was, indeed, madness. Surrender was so near, so desperately, dangerously imminent, that she could barely resist him, didn't, in fact, really want to.

'You want to as much as I do,' he whispered, the words warm against her breasts where his tongue touched so tantalisingly.

But Leith, now that her token protest had been established, could find new strength, new reserves to resist the surrender she so very much both wanted and feared.

'No,' she said, clearer, this time. And her hands regained some degree of mental control, were able to push against him, to resist despite the arguments of her compliant body. 'No, I don't want to, not now, not this way.'

'What other way is there?' And there was a dangerous undertone there in his voice. 'I want you ... you want me. Surely that's all there is to it.'

His lips trailed a fiery path up along her breasts, touched at her throat, her cheek, then retraced that path, silently pursuading in a manner no words could ever accomplish. Leith shuddered at the pleasure in the touch.

Wanting. No word of loving, needing ... only wanting. And for her, it wasn't all there was to it, not now and not ever. Without her love, a love she couldn't any longer deny, being returned, there could never be *anything* to it. And certainly not this.

Leith struggled to sit upright, thrust at him with hands now clawed into defence. 'I said no, and I meant it,' she cried, her voice almost a shriek. And with that small, brief, return to sanity, came her only defence, her best defence, and she used it fiercely, angrily.

'If this is all you want, then why not hurry home to Madeline? I'm sure you wouldn't get any arguments from her,' Leith cried, and was thrusting herself out of the car, fleeing as if the devil himself was in pursuit, before Mace Benedict could answer or even try to prevent her going. She heard only a muttered, fierce-sounding oath as she flung open the gate and then slammed it behind her, running for the safety of the house despite the fact that he hadn't so much as left the car.

He didn't leave the car. Not that she really would have expected him to, given a period of rational thought. But at that point in time, Leith was far from even instants of rational thought. She was too busy fleeing ... still fleeing from her own sensuality, from her own desires, from her love and her hate of Mace Benedict.

She slammed the door of the house behind her as she entered, and stood huddled against it, flattened against it as if she could block his entrance by her weight alone. Only of course there was nothing to block, except her own thoughts and ravaged emotions. Mace Benedict didn't come to her door.

But neither did he drive away; at least, not immediately. Despite Leith's shattered emotional state, she was aware enough to realise that he was still outside, his car unmoving. Plucking up her courage, she left the now-locked door and slunk over to peep from the darkness of the kitchen. Yes, he was there. She could see the glow of his cigarette, could even fancy he was puffing upon it angrily.

Angry? In his place, Leith knew, she'd have been more than just angry. Absolutely livid was closer to the truth of it, yet Mace just sat there. And why? Did he expect her to go out and apologise? Well he'd sit there a long, long time before that happened, she determined.

She still thought that when he finally left, although

she was mildly disappointed, somehow, with the calm, silent departure of the vehicle. No spinning of tyres, no tooting of horn, just an easy rumble of powerful engine and the swishing of his tyres as he turned through the driveway and slipped down the road like a wraith in the moonlight.

She watched for long moments after that, but she didn't cry until she'd gone out to let Snap into the house, until the pup had smothered her in kisses more loving but less moving than those she'd tried to reject from the man now gone from her life.

And it wasn't until she'd washed and got ready for bed that she realised with a start that he *wasn't* gone . . . not entirely. He'd be back the next morning—this morning, she realised with a startled look at the clock— to help Anson Jones with the fencing.

And he would come, Leith realised. Regardless of their bitter fight, regardless of how angry he might be with her, he wouldn't neglect a promise to help a neighbour.

It was morning, the morning after a nearly sleepless, soul-searching night of tossing and turning and turbulent half-awake nightmares, that Leith realised with startling clarity that she, too, would be forced to make some contribution to the day ahead. Even if it meant face-to-face encounters with Mace Benedict, as it must.

· It was, after all, *her* fence they were repairing. *Her* property they were improving, despite the short-term benefit to Anson Jones. And the very least that might be expected of her would be coffee and something to eat during their breaks. And of course lunch. During the night she'd come to the realisation that even the day before, she really should have spent less time agonising over the situation and more tending to her own role, to the simple courtesy required of her.

Leith was up, washed, dressed and had her chores attended to before the arrival of Anson Jones' battered utility was revealed by the belching blue smoke and Snap's warning barks.

By the time for morning smoko, she'd prepared a goodly quantity of fresh scones and butter tarts and was ready to take them down to the bottom paddock. Only ... where was Mace? He couldn't have arrived without her knowledge, she thought, and yet ... surely he wouldn't have abandoned Anson to the job without warning? Or maybe he would? At any rate, she was now past the point of worrying about Mace Benedict's actions.

Calling the dog to her, she lifted the immense tray of tea-time goodies and began the long stroll down to where the men had been working the day before.

It was, she decided during her walk, perhaps better that Mace hadn't arrived. No need to worry about impressions, no worries about how they might regard each other after the previous night's abortive ending. She was still thinking about that when she stepped round the corner of the track and almost walked straight into him.

'Well, this is a pleasant surprise,' said an unexpectedly calm voice. 'And just in time, too. We're more than ready for a bit of sustenance.'

Leith was so startled she might have dropped the tray, only Mace was ready for that, and had taken it from her nerveless fingers before the surprise of his presence could let her release the tray.

'Smoko, Anse!' he called loudly, and had turned away before she could speak, or even think of what she might say.

Anson Jones, as usual, said little beyond a muttered 'G'day', but he made up for it with the obvious enjoyment of her offerings. The scones and butter tarts seemed to disappear as if by magic, although the young, inarticulate grazier did manage to save a small offering to Snap, who took it with unexpected graciousness.

'Got a marvellous way with animals, that boy,' Mace said then. 'You want to give him the dog whenever he comes up to check on the sheep, and before you know it she'll be trained without even knowing it was happening. I don't think I've ever run across anyone with quite that strong a gift for dog handling.'

But this, along with other equally inconsequential discussion, was about all he said to her during smoko. No hint of apology for the incidents of the previous night, no hint either that he might expect an apology from her, or perhaps at least an explanation. And no hint of anger, or outrage, or . . . or anything. It was as if he'd divorced the incident from his mind, and Leith found herself wishing she could do the same, despite the certain knowledge that she couldn't and wouldn't . . . not ever.

His indifference only made the hurt deeper. He didn't, of course, love her, but to think she couldn't even evoke anger . . .

She found it more hurtful than anything else, but managed to keep up her end of the meagre conversation until the moment when she could collect the empty tray and accoutrements and make a relatively graceful exit.

'Lunch will be at 12:30, if that's all right,' she said then, and was both relieved and annoyed by the reply that it wasn't necessary as both men had brought sandwiches.

'You can't work all day on sandwiches . . . or at least not on my fences,' she replied pointedly. 'Twelve-thirty!' And departed, back straight and head held high, before either man could argue further. Not that Anson Jones would argue anyway, she thought on the trek back to the house, but Mace certainly would have. The tiny success gave her a satisfaction out of all proportion to the significance of the event.

By the appointed time, she was more than ready. A large roast of beef, complete with all the trimmings adorned the large table, along with a fresh load of bread that was somewhat strangely shaped but immensely pleasing for all that. It was the first time she'd managed a really acceptable bread-making in the combustion stove, and considering her mental state, Leith thought it quite marvellous despite the rather lop-sided appearance.

She'd laid out fresh towels and hand-cleaner at the laundry sink, and was just putting the final touches to her Yorkshire pudding when a soft knock at the door announced the arrival of her work crew.

'My God . . . you don't expect us to go back to work after a meal like this,' Mace said, honest wonderment written all over his face. 'I, for one, will need a four-hour nap first.'

Leith's heart sank; she'd always thought of hard-working men as having enormous fuel requirements, but had she thought wrong . . . over-done it? Then she caught the look on the face of Anson Jones, and knew that whatever Mace Benedict might think, here was one man who agreed totally with her own attitudes.

After washing up, both men tucked into the meal as if they'd not eaten in days, and Leith joined them, surprised at her own appetite. There was little conversation until the first plates had been emptied and refilled, then Mace leaned back in his chair and looked admiringly at both Leith and the half-demolished meal.

'Did you manage all this from that diabolical stove?' he asked, and Leith fairly welled up with pride when he nodded satisfaction at her affirmation. 'You're a quick study, I have to say it,' he continued. 'I've known people to take years to learn how to bake bread like this.'

Anson merely nodded his agreement and continued his assault on the remainder of the Yorkshire pudding, for all the world as if it was the last meal he'd ever manage, but Leith took only pleasure from that silent approval, as well.

Between the two men, they did a respectable job of making three-quarters of an apple pie disappear, followed by two cups of coffee each, before Mace finally called a halt and insisted they return to work while they could still walk.

As she saw the men to the door, the incident of the evening well-nigh displaced by Mace's compliments about her cooking, her managing, Leith felt on top of the world. Not that she would forget last night's incident, but at least she could now feel that perhaps it hadn't been quite as serious as it might have been, that perhaps her childish tantrum might have been over-looked.

'That was a marvellous meal, Leith,' he said, and she thought her heart would burst. Then he turned to his companion, and his next words assured it, only not as she wanted, needed.

'You don't want to stop at fixing the fences, mate,' Mace said without so much as a glance at Leith to see the effect of his next, horrifying words. 'You want to be up here courting; you won't find tucker like that everywhere today.'

Anson, to his credit, blushed silently. Leith could only gulp her heartbreak as she met Mace's mocking, soul-destroying black eyes.

What he hadn't said—out loud—was that *he* certainly *wouldn't* be courting. But he'd said it; Leith got the message loud and clear. Had it not been for the incident of the night before, she might have passed off the remark as a back-handed compliment, but the unholy glow in Mace's eyes, the cruel twist of his lip, made that quite impossible. This was no compliment; it was total rejection, cruel and meant to be cruel. Only Anson Jones, the innocent accessory to the cruelty, remained innocent of the message involved.

A fiery reply was lurking on Leith's lips, but before she could utter a single word, Mace had turned away and the two men were headed for the gate. Leith could only fume impotently, as she did at length while cleaning up after the meal and then, damnably, while preparing the necessities for afternoon smoko some time later.

And when she did take the tray down to the work area that afternoon, the atmosphere was palpably cool. True, the men were tired and rightly so, considering the tremendous amount of work they'd done, but it was more than that and both Leith and Mace Benedict knew it. Something was missing from their conversation, or else something had been added. Leith felt she sounded too cheerful, too obviously determined to ignore Mace's earlier stab. And Mace was, for him, unusually taciturn, overly remote.

She stayed only as long as she absolutely had to, unable to bear the iciness, the chill that hung between them like an enormous hail cloud. Then Leith turned her energies to gathering her mud bricks and laying out the foundation for her wood-fired kiln. It was hard work, and much, much harder to come, she knew, but at least it kept her mind occupied.

When the two men left, just before five o'clock, she forced herself to appear totally cheerful, and made a special point of thanking each of them, avoiding as she did so the cynical look in Mace's black eyes. The tears didn't come until after their dust trail had settled on the gravelly mountain road, but the evening was among the longest and most lonely of Leith's young life.

The next two weeks could have felt equally lonely, but she forced her mind to concentrate on work, forced her soul to put Mace Benedict back into perspective, to accept the defeat she had, herself, created.

She built the kiln, working from dawn to dusk each day and taking immense pleasure in the construction despite her uncertainty about its future success. She had only her own experience to help in her judgment that her duck-dam clay was sufficiently pure to withstand the enormous temperatures that must be created within the kiln, and if she turned out to have been wrong, the result would be a tremendous amount of time wasted, to say the least.

And building the kiln was only the first step. Even more time-consuming was the cutting, splitting and stacking of sufficient wood even for just a trial firing. She reckoned it would take anywhere from half a ton to a full ton of wood, all split to the variety of sizes she needed for temperature control, and all of it properly dried and seasoned.

About the only consolation was the fact that she had been able to design the kiln to take longer wood than her cantankerous combustion stove, but the effort required to collect a ton of seasoned, dry wood was nonetheless enormous.

By the end of the two weeks, Leith was sunburnt, scratched and bone-weary from the long days of preparing her wood-pile. She'd cut down every standing dead tree within reach of the tracks on her property and wasn't entirely sure that she'd be able to find the energy for a career of making wood-fired pottery full-time.

'Personally, I think you're mad as a meat axe,' Helen said when Leith stopped in for coffee and a chat to celebrate the end of her wood-preparing ordeal. 'I mean, fair enough to use wood in your stove; you've got plenty and it isn't all that hard to keep enough done to carry on with. But to cut your own wood for something that uses it at *that* rate, well, I wouldn't do it, that's a certainty.'

'The way I feel today I'm inclined to agree with you,' Leith grinned, then winced as yet another sore muscle gave a twinge of protest. 'But really, wood-firing is a luxury, in a way, the really classic way of firing top-class pottery. I just *have* to try it; more than that, I *have* to learn to do it right. And I will, too.'

'That's if you don't kill yourself first,' George interjected. 'How much pottery can you make if you're knocked over by a falling limb, or get yourself hurt? Damned stupid to be out cutting trees by yourself, that's what I say.'

'Chauvinist! You do it all the time,' Leith cried. 'Look at the enormous woodpile outside the door. You cut all that, and don't bother to tell me you had Helen hanging on your coat-tails while you did it, because I wouldn't believe you.'

'Wouldn't expect you to,' he shrugged. 'But let's not forget that I've been working in the bush all me life and I know what's what. You're just bloody lucky there hasn't been an accident, my girl. Sure, I know you can use a chain saw, but there's more to it than that and you don't know the half of it. Just the shock of the tree you've cut hitting the ground can be enough to jar loose another one right behind you if its been burned out underneath, or rotted out. You're playing with fire if you keep it up, I tell you that.'

'And I'll be playing without fire if I don't,' Leith retorted half angrily. 'I do have a stove to keep going all winter and I do have to learn these things. I just can't afford to be paying somebody else to do things I can be doing for myself; I haven't got the money.'

'Nor will you have, if a bloody great limb drops on your head,' he replied. 'Use your head, girl. You've got Mace Benedict and that young real estate chap both panting after you all the time—let *them* do your wood-cutting for you, like any sensible . . .'

'I will not!' Leith interrupted. 'I don't want to have to depend on some man "panting after me"—not for firewood or anything else. I'm my own person, damn it, and I want to stay that way.'

'Alive or dead?' George snapped, his short-fuse patience finally exhausted. 'You're mad, girl . . . mad! All this rubbish about being independent is one thing, but you go too far sometimes and this is one of them. Why, I've half a mind to speak to Mace about it—he'd damned well put a stop to . . .'

'No!' Leith shrieked. 'No . . . no . . . no . . . no . . .' Then she calmed slightly, although her own temper was close to eruption point. 'Oh, please, George . . . can't you understand? If I'm going to have to depend on Mace Benedict—or any other man for that matter—to cut my firewood and fix my fences and . . . and everything else the farm demands, then I shouldn't be here at all. I should sell up and move back to the city, where I can control my own life. It isn't right and it isn't fair to always be depending on somebody else for everything.'

'It isn't everything, you know,' Helen said softly, 'just a few things that even common sense must tell you have *some* logic. All right, so you don't want to take advantage of friendship, or romance, or whatever, but by the same token it's ridiculous to bury yourself in sheer hard labour just for the sake of doing it yourself. Really, Leith, you do carry your need for independence too far sometimes, and what I'm afraid of is that it will become a habit.'

'I don't understand,' Leith said. 'What is so wrong with being independent? I can't imagine you being very happy if I were the type who had to come running for help with every little thing.'

'No, we probably wouldn't,' Helen replied gravely. 'But you're not that type. If you were, I'm sure you'd never have bought your farm in the first place. It's just that . . . well, what about when you get married? And you will, you know. Surely you realise that marriage is a sharing thing, not some life-time battle to maintain your total independence. It's a matter of *inter*dependence, not independence.'

'Well from what I've seen—and I don't mean you, so please don't be offended—it's more usually a matter of somebody being dominant and somebody being submissive,' Leith replied hotly.

'And very good some of those marriages are, too, if they involve the right people in the right roles,' her friend replied. 'But what sort of marriage wouldn't work for you, and nobody's suggesting it should. It bloody well wouldn't work in this house, either, as I'm sure you well know. But what does work is a damned good partnership, with each of us doing our own thing, with our own sort of independence and our own sense of identity—as partners. Which means that each of us ends up being dominant, depending on the circumstances. I don't tell George how to build fences or how to cut firewood and he doesn't tell me how to run my end of the piggery or my part of the house. Or at least not often. But neither of us tries to run *everything*—and that's what you're doing, Leith, admit it or not. You're so damned busy maintaining your own independence that you won't give anybody a chance to fit into your life except totally on *your* terms.'

Helen sighed, paused then sighed again. 'Oh, hell . . . I didn't mean to pick on you, but it's true. You're at least halfway to being in love with Mace Benedict; that's obvious even to an insensitive oaf like George, here—who will never so much as *think* of mentioning one single word of this conversation,' she scowled, shooting her husband a glance so fierce, so warning, that Leith even cowered in surprise. 'But instead of giving it a chance, instead of at least trying to find out what the man's like, you spend your time fighting with him over things so damned silly that I'm surprised he bothers with you.'

'He doesn't,' Leith snapped, anger flowing in to cover the hurt that even the mention of Mace could so easily provide. 'And he won't, so please let's not talk about him, because he has nothing whatsoever to do with this. How can you possibly twist a conversation so much? We're talking about me cutting my own firewood, not about marriage or anything even remotely like it.'

'We started out talking about firewood,' Helen corrected her gently, but got no further.

'Well then there's no more to be said,' Leith cut in. 'The wood's cut, without any of George's predicted accidents, I might add, and right at this moment, for certain, my body agrees with both of you that I should never cut another bit. And I shan't, at least for quite some time. But neither shall I start taking advantage of *any* man just to get my firewood cut, not even,' she declared with a firm chin and equally firm conviction, 'Mace Benedict!'

'So what are you going to do about your wood firing?' Helen asked. 'George does have a point, you know? If it takes you a ton of wood every time you fire the kiln up, you'll spend more time cutting wood than you will potting. A lot more time.'

'Yes, of course he's right,' Leith admitted, her own temper now cooled. 'Actually, if the wood firing works as it should, and if the results are what I hope for, I might just be able to raise my prices enough that I can buy wood, although at, what, thirty dollars a ton?, it might still be quite a problem. Still, I'll face that one when I get to it. For the moment I'm just glad I've got enough for the test. And who knows—maybe the damned kiln will melt itself. It could, if I've misjudged the clay content and type in my mud-bricks.'

She left shortly thereafter, glad to have the argument ended. The last thing Leith wanted, independence or no, was a violent disagreement with people who were both friends and neighbours. As she drove down to pick up her mail, she felt mildly guilty at having mentioned buying firewood, because she had no intention—at this stage—of doing any such thing. No, she'd keep right on cutting her own as long as her strength held out, Leith thought. There were better places to expend her dwindling finances than on firewood at $30 a ton.

Then she arrived at the mailboxes, picked up her mail, and the first letter she opened relieved her of any feelings about guilt, because it almost certainly decreed that buying firewood was exactly what she would have to do, dwindling finances or not!

CHAPTER SEVEN

LEITH drove home in a daze of incredulity, and her first task upon arriving was to read the letter again . . . and yet again. Still, she could hardly believe it, despite the written evidence.

She sat at her big kitchen table, turning the heavy, embossed stationery over and over in her fingers as the implications of the letter bombarded her mind. This was her big chance; the one she'd worked for all these years, the one she'd dreamed of.

The letter was from the director of what Leith privately thought to be not only the most prestigious gallery in Melbourne, but among the finest in all of Australia. Certainly, she thought, the most influential.

And he wanted her—her, Leith Larsen—to put together a massive private exhibition for *his* gallery. An exclusive, highly-publicised, personal exhibition for the second week in December. It was just too totally, fantastically unbelievable!

It was, of course, sheer good fortune that the opening existed at all; his letter was almost comfortingly direct on that point. There had been a management error (obviously, since his bookings would normally have been made as much as a year in advance) on the part of another exhibitor, and as a result the relevant week was free—hers if she wanted it.

Wanted it? How could she even consider *not* wanting it? Leith knew craftsmen who'd *steal* for a chance like this one, considering that a successful exhibition under this gallery's sponsorship was almost a gilt-edged invitation to national fame. For someone in Leith's position, it could be the gateway to true recognition, and more important, the gateway to the kind of financial success that would guarantee her independence for years to come.

But it would take work, hard work and plenty of it. She had only a few true exhibition pieces in their completed state, and most of those ready for firing were geared to the peculiarities of the wood-fired kiln.

Dared she chance any potential exhibition piece to the unknown risks of a technique she understood only in theory? And yet, if the wood-firing test was successful, how could she not dare? It would present a definite step forward, an indication of the artistry that formed the core of her entire potter's mentality.

'Well personally, I think you're daft if you do,' Helen said when faced with the question the next day. 'Think of the work involved, not to mention the risks. If you lost some of your best potential work to a chancy thing like that, you'd be heartbroken, not to mention the time factors involved.'

'And if I didn't take the chance I'd risk going to the exhibition without—maybe—some of the best work I've ever done,' Leith replied. 'No, I've got to try it. It just means I'll have to do even more, to cover the possible failures, that's all. I spoke to the gallery by telephone yesterday, and they've room for anywhere from twenty-five to seventy-five individual pieces. I can manage the minimum now, in a pinch, so everything that comes out of the kiln with exhibition quality gives me that much more final choice. I *can* do it, Helen. And I'm going to.'

'You've only got two months.'

'All the more reason to try my tests with the wood kiln as soon as possible,' Leith said. 'If it provides the glazing results that I think it will—that it *must*—then I'm home and hosed. If not, I've got the electric kiln to fall back on, and some special glazing effects that I've just about perfected.'

'Well you can count on me for any help I can give, although I tell you now that I draw the line at cutting your firewood,' Helen smiled. 'And since apart from that, I suspect there's little I could do, maybe best I just trot off home and leave you to it, eh?'

'No, there's one other thing,' Leith said, almost

sheepishly. 'You could lend me the chauvinist piggy bank, if you wouldn't mind.'

'For the exhibition?'

'Of course. It's really an exhibition piece . . . oh, not because of the, uhm, rather unique facial characteristics, but the glazing turned out just right, for the effect I was looking for. Of course, it wouldn't be for sale or anything, and I'd make special arrangements for the shipping and . . .'

'Good Lord, stop it,' her friend interjected. 'Of course you can take it along. It's just that, well, if it's that good, shouldn't you be offering it for sale? I mean . . .'

'Now who's being ridiculous?' Leith cut in. 'Of course it can't be for sale. It's yours, for goodness' sake. And it was a gift because, well, you know very well why. I wouldn't have nearly the value to anyone else anyway and besides, I wanted you to have it and I still do. But it would go well in the exhibition because I very seldom do anything like it.'

'Right, that's settled then,' said Helen. 'Now I'm off home and I expect not to see you until you can show me the results of your firing tests. And, after you've got a decent night's sleep later, because I know you—you'll be exhausted almost beyond repair.'

Truer words were never spoken. After forty-eight hours without sleep, hours in which Leith seemed chained to the enormous wood-fired kiln, hours in which her arms and shoulders turned to one enormous ache, her eyes burning with exhaustion and the strain of trying to peep through the spy-hole to ensure accurate temperatures by way of the strategically placed Seger cones inside the kiln, she literally collapsed into her bed when her judgment and instincts told her the firing was complete.

She slept almost entirely through the next twenty-four hours, then fussed and fidgeted through the next three days as she impatiently waited for the moment when she dared open the kiln and see first-hand the results of her attempted firing. It was a wait of such intense impatience that she was almost as exhausted when it came time to open the kiln as she'd been immediately after the firing.

Her fingers trembled almost uncontrollably. She had, at one point, to force herself to stop, to take several deep, slow breaths before reaching in to lift each individual piece of fragile pottery from the kiln, her fingers gentle through the layers of ash that disguised the final accuracy of her judgment.

There were the usual, expectable problem pieces. Pieces where the fragile glaze had faulted, fractured, crazed into a mass of nearly invisible but none the less heart-stopping cracks. The few broken pieces, destroyed by some element of the firing beyond Leith's control.

But generally, despite the higher-than-expected rate of failures, the result was astonishing. Colours totally alive in their brilliance, effects both expected and truly unexpected, unexplainable, yet superb. She had only included five possible exhibition pieces in the test firing, not daring to trust too many to a technique she didn't fully understand. But when the pieces were cleaned, carefully and gently, there were *seven* items so superb, so individually excellent that she had to gasp at her luck.

On one deceptively simple platter, the melting glaze had flowed exactly as expected, then flowed that infinitesimal bit further to create not only the effect Leith had wanted, but something greater, minutely closer to unattainable perfection and yet almost magical in the result.

And in another, moulded and sculpted from the very clay of her duck dam, impurities in the clay had totally altered the effects of the glaze; indeed the entire shape of the piece had been altered, slightly melted by the intense heat and its melding with the glaze. The result, totally unexpected, unexpectable, was superb.

But most important, she'd found in one simple, arduous testing that she could handle the wood-fired kiln, that it would create the types of effects she wanted. Perfecting the technique might take years, but this, at least, was a phenomenally encouraging beginning.

Leith was first ecstatic, then exhausted. The nervous

strain—now relieved by her success—retreated to leave her feeling light-headed, hollow in the stomach, physically debilitated beyond all logic. It was all she could do to stumble back to the house, shamble through the motions of a much-needed shower, and fling herself into bed. And once there, she found sleep an elusive dream as her mind flowed like an errant river, touching on designs, mentally fingering the moist, pliant clay, calculating the mix of glazes. The rest that finally came was fretful, nerve-struck.

In the morning, she could barely slow herself down long enough to gulp down a meagre breakfast and feed her livestock. The clay was now calling in a siren song, irresistible. She worked through without pause until dark, only just remembered her ducks and chickens in time to fling out hasty handfuls of grain, had to feed Snap in the kitchen, guilty at the small dog's uncomplaining yet obvious hunger.

Her sleep was equally turbulent that night, and the following day she rushed into the nearest shop where she could purchase several flood-lights, then spent an exasperating hour rigging them through a jumble of extension cords until she had the light she needed.

That night she didn't sleep at all. She was working in a frenzy, her fingers so attuned to the clay, to her dreams, to something totally intangible and yet equally so real she could feel it, that she didn't need sleep, couldn't spare the time. It seemed as if hands and mind had become separate entities, and she sculpted clay while her mind was engaged in planning the glazes for it even before the final shape was established.

A ruthlessness crept into her work; things that didn't go exactly right were exorcised without thought, without question. Only the best could survive, only the best could even warrant the thought of completion. Her efforts swung wildly between the safety of known colours, known techniques, and insanely experimental attempts whose results could only be guessed at, prayed for.

During the next few days, she didn't go to bed at all, but grabbed cat-naps whenever exhaustion forced them upon her. She ate only things that could be bolted down without the time wasted in preparation, cheeses, bread, crackers and various cooked sausages.

The electric kiln was in constant use. No sooner would it cool down sufficiently from one biscuit firing so that she could unload it, than it would be loaded up again and pushed to maximum temperature. On the rare occasions when Leith bothered to think about it, the power bill she must be accumulating was staggeringly fearsome. Only she didn't think about that often; it wasn't relevant in any event. All that counted was her work, the all-encompassing creativity that thrust aside any other consideration.

Helen came by one day, only to find Leith hunched over her workbench, a cold cup of coffee growing colder on one corner and a stale sandwich squatting dejectedly at the other.

'My God!' she cried. 'When's the last time you had a decent meal, Leith? You look like death warmed over.'

'I don't know,' Leith replied, reaching absently with one clay-smeared hand to brush back a straggling lock of hair from her eyes. 'Does it matter?'

'Not if you're planning a posthumous exhibition,' Helen replied, but the comment was lost. Leith wasn't really listening, and although she heard the words, their meaning tumbled emptily across the frothing crests of her own thoughts.

'Leith!' The outcry drew only a querulous 'What?', and when Helen repeated her query about food, Leith merely shrugged the question aside.

'I'm not hungry right now,' she growled, not bothering to add that really she didn't know if she was or not; it just wasn't important enough to consider ... not now. Now, she must concentrate on the living clay before her, concentrate on imparting that magic something which lurked in her fingers, seeking escape to the malleable clay.

Still, when Helen finally left her with an exclamation of anger and disgust, only to return sometime later with fresh coffee and a platter of fresh sandwiches, Leith allowed her friend to browbeat her into pausing long enough to consume them. But their conversation during the short break was scanty; Leith's mind was still locked in her work, and she couldn't or wouldn't break it free for small talk.

'You can't keep this up,' Helen said, stern in her obvious concern for Leith's health. But the concern was wasted.

'I'm all right,' Leith retorted. 'I'm not tired and I'm not hungry and I do wish you'd stop worrying, because there's nothing wrong. I'm always like this when I'm working at my best.' This, she knew, wasn't at all true, but if it would ease Helen's mind, then the white lie wouldn't hurt at all. Anything to get her friend to just go away and let Leith continue with her work.

'You're overtired, and I'll bet you've not had a decent meal since you heard about the exhibition,' Helen insisted. 'Please, Leith . . . give it a rest for today, at least. The firewood you wanted me to order for you will be arriving this afternoon, so you'd have to devote tomorrow to stacking it anyway; what difference can half a day make?'

'All the difference in the world,' Leith replied hotly, but the damage was done, now. Her mind had been subtly side-tracked, and now had opened to allow thoughts of the four tonnes of firewood she'd had Helen order for her. All dry, east-coast peppermint—at a price that decimated the remains of her spare cash, but it would be worth it . . . worth every single penny if she could manage two more wood firings before the exhibition.

'I'll come and give you a hand after I've fed out in the morning,' Helen said, 'but only if you promise me you'll stop early today and try to get some proper sleep.'

'Oh, all right,' Leith agreed, not meaning a word of it. 'I'll stop at . . . four o'clock, for sure.'

A safe enough promise—Helen would be busy by that time feeding her pigs; she wouldn't be able to check without breaking into her own rigid routine. Only

Helen wasn't to be taken in. She hadn't, as had Leith, gone days without proper nutrition or sleep, and the ploy was transparent as glass to her.

'You're fooling nobody, Missy,' she said threateningly, 'least of all me. Now you listen! That firewood will be coming first thing this afternoon, and I'm coming over then as well. So you'll quit working once it's all been delivered ... quit working, have a long shower, a decent meal and get to bed—or else, damn it, I'll leave the job of sorting and stacking the wood all to you. Either way, you'll end up losing the same amount of time, so you might as well take the time to get some rest.'

Leith looked at her, petulance written all over her face. 'Oh ...' she started out, only to be interrupted by a stern command.

'Oh ... nothing. Damn it, Leith—you'll only end up making some stupid mistake and ruining some potentially good work if you don't take care of yourself. Even you must be able to see that. Now is it a bargain?'

'Yes,' Leith replied without hesitation. She knew Helen was right, and besides, her concentration was broken, now. 'In fact, I'll go one better. I'll quit for the day *now* and go have a nap. How's that?'

'It would be marvellous if I didn't think you'd take it as an excuse to stay up and work all night,' Helen said. 'So be warned, young lady. Tonight I'm going to be keeping an eye on you, and if I catch you at it, well, there'll be trouble, I promise.'

And her stern determination hadn't abated one whit by that afternoon, when she arrived hard on the heels of the truckload of wood to find Leith looking only slightly refreshed despite a three-hour nap.

'I think you should come to us for dinner tonight,' she said after the wood was unloaded into an enormous, untidy pile outside the pottery. 'At least that way I'll be sure of getting one decent meal into you before you bury yourself in your work again.'

'So you can spend the evening lecturing me, you mean,' Leith replied with a grin. 'Well, thanks but no thanks. I'm just going to make a start at sorting this wood, and then I'm going to follow your first orders—shower, food and to bed. You've got enough to do at home without worrying about me, and I've got too much to do here to be much of a dinner guest, I'm afraid.'

'All right, then we'll both make a start on it. But when I quit, so do you,' Helen replied calmly. 'And if I find you've so much as stacked one extra piece before I get back tomorrow morning, then heaven help you, because I'll really be upset, Leith. I mean that.'

'I promise that I'll quit when you do, and that I'll have a really early night tonight,' Leith said. 'But if you think I'm waiting until you arrive tomorrow to get stuck into that wood-pile, then you've got another think coming, because I'm starting bright and early.'

Despite her best intentions, however, it didn't quite work out that way. After Helen left, Leith had conscientiously returned to the house, luxuriated in a long shower, cooked herself an enormous omelette and then gone to bed even before the sun. In her more rational thoughts, she even agreed with Helen; she *had* been overdoing things. But once she'd had seven hours of sleep, her body simply didn't need any more, and she was wide awake at midnight with her best intentions adrift by moonlight as she tossed a mental coin—wood-pile or pottery?

When Helen drove up at morning tea time, it was to find the wood all sorted and stacked, and Leith once again elbow deep in moist clay, her attention fully focussed on what she was doing.

'Before you start, let me say that I had ten hours sleep, a shower and a good meal,' Leith cautioned. It wasn't quite a lie, if she counted the nap earlier that day. 'So don't hassle me, please, Helen. I'm fresh as a daisy and fit as a fiddle.'

'And mad as a meat-axe,' her friend commented drily. 'But it's your life; I'm not going to give myself ulcers worrying about you.'

'Good, because there's nothing to worry about,'

Leith replied absently. 'All I need is another week or so, and I'll be ready for my first *real* wood firing. And if I'm lucky, and get enough done, I might even get in a second one before the deadline.' She was already planning for that; there was nearly enough really good work on hand for that first firing, and if she could just keep up the momentum, she'd be more than ready for the exhibition and have a few pieces for general sale as well.

Plunging back into the moulding of a specially intricate piece, she hardly even noticed Helen's departure, much less the determined, yet speculative look on her friend's face.

By the end of the day she was back into her routine, pausing only often enough to feed the animals and occasionally grab something to nibble on herself. She worked right through the night, ignoring the heaviness of her eyes, the disapproving twinges of muscle-ache and the fluttering of taut, over-strained nerves.

In the morning, she drove into Hobart early, begrudging every minute of the trip, but desperately in need of new glazing materials, ordered a month earlier and vital to her plans. By noon she was back in the pottery, and at midnight she was still there, cat-napping at her work bench beside an empty coffee cup and another stale sandwich.

On Helen's next visit, nearly a week later, Leith thought herself lucky to have been just finishing a quick meal when Helen arrived.

'I've just got up,' she said, truthfully, but couldn't help adding a not-so-white lie by adding, 'And I feel just great. I had a really good night's sleep.' In fact, she'd slept all of two hours.

Ignoring Helen's rather sceptical glance, she escorted her friend to the pottery, now almost overflowing with pieces ready for firing in one kiln or the other.

'Come and see how much I've done,' Leith said, excited. 'Another few days—maybe even by tomorrow— and I'll be ready for another go at the wood kiln.'

'A go at a pine box is more likely,' Helen growled,

not at all deceived by Leith's bright patter. It was obvious, both from the accumulation of finished work and Leith's general demeanor, that she'd been working steadily and without proper rest since the last visit.

And Leith knew she wasn't deceived, but she managed to ignore the prospect in her own excitement at showing Helen the various exhibition possibilities she had created.

'If I can get two good wood firings, I'll have more than enough,' she chattered. 'And I will, somehow. But, oh, the time's running out. There's less than three weeks before I have to be in Melbourne and I want to try and make one firing go four days, if I can, just to see what the extra accumulation of ash does.'

In her exhausted nerviness, she hardly noticed that Helen seemed hardly to be paying any attention, but was instead concentrating on a deliberate assessment of Leith's haggard expression, her hollowed cheeks and wide, almost glassy eyes. As before, Helen's departure went almost unnoticed as she plunged back into her work, and she never left the workshop even for coffee during the rest of the day.

By late afternoon she was finished but for one, final effort, and in her exhausted, feverish mind she was no longer certain if this was truly a possible exhibition piece or some grotesque flight of fancy sent to plague her throughout the preparation for the exhibition.

Certainly it had endured through almost all of the time she'd spent, coming off the shelf to be unwrapped from its damp wrappings for detailing that sometimes involved only the slightest touch of a wooden spatula, or the gentlest brush of a finger-tip, but at other times involved almost a complete revision.

When—if—it was completed, Leith knew, it might be either the *pièce de résistance* of her entire exhibition or something so innately personal and private that it would never leave her hands. What she did know was that she absolutely *had* to finish it, *had* to include it in the wood firing.

And later, as she stared at the work through eyes

fever-bright with tiredness and strain, Leith was forced to wonder if her own emotions were not playing cruel tricks on her. Her fingers played softly on the still-pliant clay, touching lightly at the familiar features, the life-sized bust of Mace Benedict now perfect in every detail.

Once placed in the electric kiln for slow, steady biscuit firing, the internal wax plug on which the bust had been moulded would melt away, leaving her with the still-painstaking job of glazing the bust for its final firing in the wood kiln. It was not a technique she often used, risky in the extreme, but throughout her muse-driven creative period since she'd been informed of the exhibition, this single piece of work had drawn her like a moth to the flame. She was loathe to stop perfecting it, gaining some tangible pleasure from the touch of it, the look of that face as her facile fingers had crafted each detail.

But now it was done. Must be done, because she was running out of time. Tomorrow she would begin loading the wood kiln for its first real firing, the next day—or maybe even tomorrow night—she would start that firing, beginning forty-eight hours of constant supervision and attention, maybe even seventy-two hours, if she could manage that long.

As long again for the kiln to cool ... plan on twice as long a time as for the firing itself, and then she could start it up again for the final time before the exhibition. But now ... now she must start the bust on its long journey through the rest of the process, must begin the slow firing to melt away the wax innards, gradually build that up to bring the bust to biscuit stage, and then begin the delicate glazing that would make or break the experiment completely.

Carefully, almost reverently, she placed the bust into the electric kiln, checked that her modifications, specially designed to carry off the melting wax, were in place. Then she carefully placed her Seger cones, unwilling to trust the pyrometer alone. A final check and she was convinced that all was ready. She could begin.

Leith determined to bring up the temperature at one-hour intervals, so that the clay would become totally free of melted wax well before the temperature became so hot that it would begin to lose the free water content. All in all, it was a chancy business; if the wax didn't melt and run away freely, if even the tiniest bit remained when the kiln temperatures reached their highest, the result would be disastrous.

So she began with the lowest setting possible, and after setting her timer, began to clean up the pottery. She would do no more potting work now, but instead would concentrate purely on the firings and on the exhaustive packing that would be required to get her work safely to Melbourne and—for some pieces—back again.

At the end of the first hour, however, she abandoned even the cleanup attempt. It seemed as if all she'd done was shift rubbish from one place to another, and the place looked, if anything, messier than when she'd begun.

Worse, fatigue was beginning to overwhelm her; Leith could feel her eyes drooping, and aching muscles cried out for relief. When she bent down, it was a tortuous effort to straighten, and she didn't dare close her eyes lest she fall asleep right where she stood.

And she couldn't do that. In hindsight, it was stupid to have put the bust into the kiln; she ought to have waited until morning, ought to have stopped, gone to bed, rested. But she hadn't, and now she *couldn't*. The biscuit firing couldn't be halted with the risk of disaster, so she'd have to stay awake somehow and see it through.

But once she'd turned up the temperature for the second time, she had an hour in which to at least make herself some coffee, perhaps even take a shower, anything to help her keep awake for the duration, she thought, sagging in the lawn chair where her boneless body slouched like some rag doll.

She thought about getting up, her thoughts sluggish as her eyelids drooped, thought about coffee, could even taste it. And woke to the buzz of the timer—another hour gone.

As she bent to readjust the temperature yet again, she peered into the spyhole of the kiln although she knew it was too early yet for the Seger cones to be affected; that would come at the highest heat, when the biscuit firing was complete. But in the glare of the kiln she could just glimpse the shape of her most precious creation, and sighed deeply with the realisation that, as yet, no disaster had occurred.

The bust was still intact, the features dim in the glare, and yet obviously not sagging, not becoming deformed. In fact, it seemed at one instant as if the figure was looking back at her, the hooded eyes alive with the radiated heat, the generous mouth almost grinning.

Leith smiled to herself, subconsciously reciting the words of the immortal Robert Service poem, *The Cremation of Sam McGee.* A long way from the arctic, she thought, but wondered, somewhat irreverently, what the image in her furnace might say if she were to open the door.

'What the bloody hell...'

She started, then relaxed and muttered at the kiln. 'That's not fair; I haven't even opened the door.' And laughed, a tinkling, brittle laugh that reflected her taut nerves.

'Have you gone completely mad, woman?' And this time she had to accept the voice; it was accompanied by icy fingers that clamped on to her shoulders, lifting her and turning her to face an image of Mace Benedict that was neither warm nor smiling, but cold with barely-subdued rage.

'My God,' he grated, his eyes racing across her face, taking in every detail of her exhaustion, of the nervous strain that made her hollow-eyed, wild-eyed, strung out with tension from within. 'What the hell have you done to yourself?'

'I've been working,' she replied calmly. 'And you're not supposed to shout, you're supposed to tell me to close the door, because you're finally warm...'

'You *have* gone mad,' he hissed, eyes widening in shocked amazement. 'What in the devil are you talking about?'

'It's all right,' she said, her voice languid as her body sagged against him and her mind hung suspended between reality and the fantasy of the poem, 'I won't open the door; you won't be cold.'

Mace's grip tightened, and the severity of it brought pain and a sudden return to reality. Leith shrugged against the harshness of his fingers, her eyes blazing now as she met his gaze.

'What do you think you're doing?' she cried angrily. 'Let go of me!'

'Why? So you can spout some more utter nonsense at me?' Mace's voice was low, but grating with tension. He slackened his grip enough that it no longer hurt her, but he didn't let her go.

'I'll spout whatever I like,' she retorted. 'Now let me go! Damn you; how dare you come in here and . . . and . . .' She stammered, unable to get her tongue working properly.

Mace didn't let her go. He stood there, holding her gently but firmly, denying any escape, as his eyes ranged around the interior of the pottery. Then he looked again at Leith, and shook his head, mouth twisted in what might have been compassion.

'How long have you been going without sleep?' he demanded. And didn't wait for a reply. 'Days, from the look of you. Weeks, maybe. Hell, you look like something the cat dragged in at midnight.'

'Well, thank you very much,' Leith snapped, still twisting vainly against his grip. 'You don't look so damned spectacular yourself. Now would you mind telling me what in hell you're doing here?' Her voice was rising to a screech in her frustration at not being able to free herself, but Mace calmly took it as just another sign of hysteria.

'I came to try and talk some sense into you, since nobody else seems able to,' he snarled. 'And now I can understand why.'

'And just what's that supposed to mean?' she demanded, no longer bothering to struggle, but waiting for the moment when he must slacken his grip, so that she could take immediate advantage.

'Later,' he replied brusquely. 'For now, you're going to stop this nonsense and come to bed, before you drive yourself round the twist entirely. And I don't want any arguments, either.'

He was already turning her towards the doorway when Leith screamed at him, kicking out and struggling with all her strength. 'No ... no!' she cried. 'I can't ... oh, damn you ... why can't you just leave me alone?'

'Because you're obviously not safe to be left alone,' he replied, not ceasing his calm retreat and taking her along with him despite her protests and cries.

'But I can't go *now*,' she shouted. 'I've got stuff in the kiln, you fool. I can't just go off and leave it; it has to be regulated.'

'So regulate it,' Mace replied, thankfully pausing long enough to give her the impression he might be listening. 'But don't take all night about it.' And still he made no effort to release her. 'Better still, show *me* how, quickly, and I'll do it for you. You need your sleep more than you need another bloody pot.'

'Oh, please,' she pleaded. 'It isn't something I can just show you; it's complicated and besides, I want to do it myself. I *have* to do it myself. It'll only take another couple of hours, honestly.'

'Another couple of *hours!*' The words literally exploded from him, and the gesture seemed, somehow, to reduce the pressure of his anger. He paused momentarily, and when he spoke again his voice was calm, reasoned. 'Leith, when I came in here, you were hallucinating. In another couple of hours you won't be fit to regulate yourself, much less that damned kiln. Why not let it go? Good lord, woman, look at yourself. You're strung out like ... well ... you can't possibly keep it up, that's what I'm saying. It just isn't worth it.'

'Maybe not to you, but it certainly is to me,' she replied, calm herself, now. 'And you're not making it any easier by shouting threats and dragging me around by the arms. Now please, Mace ... I'm all right and I'm going to stay all right. If you don't believe me, you can stay and make sure ... but I am going to finish this!'

'You'll more likely finish yourself,' he growled. But he did release her, easing her gently back into her seat as if he were afraid that if he let her go suddenly, she might fall. Which, Leith thought to herself, wasn't far from the truth.

'Thank you,' she said. 'And now that we've got that much under control, perhaps you wouldn't mind explaining what you're doing here in the first place— although I think I can guess at that.'

'Well, I wouldn't want to mention any names, but some of your friends do worry about you,' he said quietly.

'And of course it would never occur to Helen that I am fully grown up now, and that I'm quite capable of managing without any of this ... this ...' Leith stammered over the rest, torn between her anger at the interference and her unarguable pleasure that Helen cared enough to risk the certainty of Leith's anger.

'What would occur to anyone with half an eye is that you've been pushing yourself too hard,' he replied, 'and since you didn't seem inclined to listen to sweet reason, well ...'

'I hardly think brute force is a viable alternative,' Leith retorted.

'If it had been, you'd be in bed right now, and staying there if I had to tie you down—or get in with you,' he replied with a slow grin. 'But unlike some people I could mention, I'm a very reasonable type—so long as you behave yourself.'

'Which I have every intention of doing,' Leith said. 'And I promise, as soon as I've got this last bit done, that I will go to bed and stay there ... alone.'

A point, she realised, that hadn't needed to be made. Mace had been having her on, deliberately goading her. He hadn't meant that part of the threat, had he?

'That's the problem with being too reasonable, all

those lost opportunities,' he grinned, then grinned even wider at the sure knowledge that he'd accurately guessed her thoughts.

'But seriously, can't you show me what it is you're aiming for? Then maybe you could grab a nap while we're waiting. I'll promise to wake you whenever you say.'

Leith was hesitant, but her exhaustion was obvious enough even to her. She quickly ran through the significance of the Seger cones, explaining that he must wake her immediately the first one began to slump. Mace repeated her instructions, again promised to wake her promptly, and Leith was thinking it wouldn't matter anyway because she couldn't possibly sleep when his gentle nudge nearly an hour later brought her bolt upright in the chair.

'For somebody who couldn't possibly sleep, you put up a pretty fair imitation,' he said with a grin. 'Anyway, your funny little pyramid thing has just decided to bend over backwards. Does this mean we can quit now?'

'Soon,' Leith replied. But it was another half an hour before the final cone revealed that she had the temperature exactly where she'd wanted it.

'Right. That's done,' she sighed, turning off the kiln in a single, flamboyant gesture. 'And now, I shall go to bed and sleep for about three days, and you can go tell Helen she can stop worrying about me.'

'I couldn't lie to the poor woman like that,' Mace replied, his eyes revealing the concern her friend must have expressed. 'But I will help you shut things up down here, and then we'll go see if you've bothered to keep enough fire in the stove so you'll have hot water for your shower.'

And despite Leith's objections, he blithely insisted on doing exactly that, collecting an enormous armload of stove wood as he passed the wood pile and then taking over her kitchen while paying absolutely no attention to her objections.

'You will go shower. Then you will come and have some soup. And then you will go to bed,' he said. 'You will not argue.'

'I just wish you'd make up your mind,' Leith complained. 'When you got here, all you wanted was for me to quit work and get some sleep, but now you keep throwing all these other things at me. I don't want a shower and I'm not hungry. Now I *do* want to go and sleep, so why don't you just let me?'

'Because I don't trust you,' he replied. 'Now stop arguing and do what you're told ... unless you'd rather I came along and helped.'

It was enough of a threat. Whatever else, Leith was in no shape to risk such action from Mace Benedict. He might only be kidding, but she knew that her own reactions wouldn't be nearly so simple. Tired as she was, she could feel herself responding to his sheer physical magnetism, and that was something she simply dared not do.

'Damn Helen anyway,' she muttered to herself as she stood and let the warmth of the shower soak into her neck and shoulders. It was one thing for her friend to be concerned, but involving Mace—deliberately involving him despite knowing how Leith would react—was very nearly inexcuseable despite the good intentions involved.

And now that he had stepped into the picture, how could she get rid of him and that as soon as possible? Obviously, she thought, by meekly following orders. She would finish her shower, eat the soup he made if it choked her, and then ... well ... then she'd see. It would be just like him to start adding on further conditions as the fancy took him.

Only he didn't. Instead, he merely shared the soup with her in silence, although he could hardly have missed noticing that Leith could barely keep awake long enough to finish it, then pointed her towards her bedroom, his expression defying objection.

Then it softened perceptively, and he reached out to clasp Leith very gently by the shoulders as she paused in the doorway. His lips were cool, almost dispassionate, as he kissed her lightly on the forehead, but his eyes were alive with suppressed laughter.

'I won't bother to join you, because I think you're too tired to notice, and that would be a waste,' he chuckled. 'So off you go, like a good little girl, and if you're especially good, perhaps I'll come tell you a bedtime story next time.'

'What next time?' she asked, already half asleep. 'You have to go now ... can't stay here.'

'Get to bed before you go to sleep standing here,' he replied with mock gruffness. 'I'll go when I'm good and ready, and certainly not before I've done the dishes. Now move ... before I decide to carry you.'

He turned away, lips pursed around a rather tuneless whistle that echoed through the brief moment it took Leith to stretch out on her bed and drift into sleep. And she heard it still when she woke to the sunshine streaming into her window and the strident cacophony of her ducks screaming to be fed. Only this time the sound was passing outside the window, and she peered through the curtain to see Mace's tall figure striding towards the old barn, Snap frolicking at his heels. A moment later, the ducks stopped their chorus, and she realised he'd halted the noise by throwing out handfuls of food for them.

The nerve! As Leith scrambled out of bed, thrusting into her robe and shaking her tousled hair into a semblance of order, she felt herself torn between anger and sheer bewilderment. Had he really stayed the night? Sleeping ... where? She'd had the only bed and she was morally certain he hadn't ... wouldn't, surely ... decided to share it with her once she was asleep

'Not that I'd have noticed, I suppose,' she muttered half aloud, then her grey eyes flashed wide open at the realisation that she *wouldn't* have noticed, not as tired as she'd been. Mace's own words came back to her: 'that would be a waste', and she shivered at how right that statement sounded now.

The whistling told her he was returning, and she strode into the kitchen just as he and the dog entered from outside.

'And how do we feel this morning?' Mace asked with a broad grin, 'awake enough for breakfast?'

'Where did you sleep last night?' It was a brusque reply, and not what she'd intended to say at all, but the words had been on the tip of her tongue, and out they came.

'Very well, thank you,' he grinned, deliberately twisting her question to suit himself. 'Scrambled eggs and bacon okay? Or do you prefer something less substantial?'

'I'd prefer to know where you slept last night,' Leith replied stolidly, standing her ground, meeting his grin without sharing it. Mace only grinned wider.

'Well,' he drawled, 'I could have slept with *you*, I suppose, but did I? That's what you really want to know, isn't it? Given the right answer to that question, you wouldn't much care if I'd slept out in the paddock with the sheep, or shared Snap's kennel.'

'That's . . . that's not true at all,' Leith replied, now cautious with her words. 'It's just that, well, there is only one bed here, and, well . . .' Her words dragged as he stepped closer, capturing her gaze with black eyes that mocked her, glittered with laughter as he reached out to cup her chin gently in one hand.

His fingertips probed lightly at the throbbing pulse in her throat, a gesture that was both caress and cool assessment. 'Do you mean to try and tell me that your concern is only for my comfort . . . or lack of it?' he chuckled.

'I don't see what's so unreasonable about that,' Leith replied, hedging, now, more aware of the touch of Mace's fingers at her throat than of any particular conversational direction. His fingers were cool against her skin, yet seemed to scorch with their own special fire, like burning ice.

'And what if I had shared your bed last night?' he asked, voice velvet soft, compelling. 'Would you mind so very much, depending, of course, on just how intimately I shared it?' And his voice lingered over *intimately* bringing the word to vibrant life as his fingers lingered at her throat.

'I ... I ... oh, stop that,' she cried as his fingers shifted lower, touching now at the first swellings of her breasts, easily parting the loose throat of the robe. Her hand flew up to stop him, but once she'd clasped his wrist, her attempts to shove it away were futile. It was like pushing at an iron bar.

'What's the matter?' he whispered. 'Too intimate? Surely not nearly as ... intimate ... as sharing a bed, dear Leith.'

'You ... I ... we didn't,' she stammered. 'You're just teasing me, although I can't think why.' She *knew* why, and knew that somehow she must put an end to this teasing before it got completely out of hand. Even if she had shared her bed with him last night—had she?—it would have been in innocence. But in his touch now there was no innocence, not in his touch, nor in her body's slow reaction to it. No innocence, only a smouldering core of desire that could explode in seconds ... or hours. That would be at *his* convenience, if she dared let him continue.

Only ... his touch had a magnetic quality she couldn't quite break. It was as if his fingers held her throat instead of merely touching there; staring into his black, black eyes was like standing on a high cliff and looking down.

'Are you sure we didn't?' he asked softly, still holding her gaze. 'You were that tired last night I doubt you'd know what might have happened. Maybe ... maybe I took advantage of you in your sleep.'

That broke the spell, as Leith was sure he knew it would. She laughed, couldn't help it. The thought of losing her virginity while asleep was just too much to take seriously.

And even more ludicrous was the possibility that Mace Benedict would be the person to take such advantage. It just wasn't, she knew, his style at all.

'That really would have been a waste,' she laughed, now able to step away from his lingering caress, now able to walk easily across the room, to turn on the electric kettle, regain some control of her body as well as her kitchen. 'Certainly it's too wild a theory to be considered without my morning coffee.'

And the tension wisped away like the steam that quickly rose from the kettle. Leith shrugged her robe more closely tight at the throat, glad that her body was otherwise concealed by its voluminous folds, and directed Mace to seat himself across the table from her.

'If you're expecting a typically mammoth farm breakfast, you'll have to go home, or at least to George and Helen's,' she said. 'I generally make do with toast and coffee, so there's nothing else out.'

He merely grinned, then directed her gaze to the opposite side of the sink where a packet of bacon sat amidst half a dozen eggs. Fresh eggs; he'd really been a busy lad this morning, Leith thought. And very competent as well, since she seldom managed to find that many on any given morning. Her chickens were still much too cagey to lay their eggs in easy-to-locate places.

'Too much to do today for any skimpy breakfasts,' he said then. 'So I ... anticipated your attitude and sort of made allowances.'

Fifteen minutes later, Leith was glad he had done so, although she was equally determined not to let him know it. Not that a verbal admission was required, she thought, considering the quantity of breakfast she'd consumed. Mace still sat across from her, sipping at his third cup of coffee and surreptitiously slipping bits of bacon rind to the eager pup under the table at his feet.

Leith sipped at her own coffee, glancing across the table from beneath lowered eyelids and wondering at the apparent domestic harmony the scene portrayed. How was it possible, she wondered, for this man to rouse her most vivid emotions one minute, yet be so strangely calming the next? And why did he bother with either one? He must surely have more important things to do than hang about organising her life for her.

'Some days I do,' he replied to her direct question, 'but this isn't one of them. Besides, I find it interesting sometimes, just trying to figure out what makes you tick.'

'Right now—work,' Leith replied. 'I have a tremendous amount to do, and very little time left.'

'And you want me to go away and leave you to it,' he said, which she had to admit wasn't really true. She didn't want him to go away; and was indeed only too ready to have him stay. Far too ready, from the viewpoint of her own common sense, Leith thought.

And yet, if she were going to get any work done today, she must get rid of him somehow. It was unthinkable, just for starters, to consider opening the electric kiln with him there. No, not ever that. Mace Benedict might, conceivably, someday see the bust she'd done of him, but he certainly couldn't be allowed to see it half finished. And besides, she found his very presence so disturbing that she knew it would be next to impossible to concentrate with him there.

'This Melbourne exhibition is very important to you, I gather,' he said, and Leith didn't bother to enquire how he knew so much about it; as he'd once said, there were no secrets in the country.

'It is,' she admitted. 'It could easily be the most important exhibition I've ever held.'

'And how will you cope with being rich and famous?' The remark stirred her alertness, but she saw immediately that he wasn't laughing at her. His question was serious.

'Hardly rich and famous,' she replied with a grin, 'although with any luck, it could certainly help finance another year or so of . . .' And she faltered on the final word, not intentionally but . . . somehow . . . she found the word tasted wrong. Mace had no such problem.

'Independence?' he said, and Leith didn't like the twist of his lip as the word emerged. 'Is that really all you want out of life, Leith . . . this ability to withdraw, to hide up here on this mountain like some latter-day bushranger?'

'I think you're rather exaggerating,' she replied, wishing he'd change the subject, get the conversation to safer ground. This was an argument neither of them could win, but one she could only lose by being involved in too long. So she tried to get out of it quickly, keeping her voice light as she said, 'but it doesn't matter, because I've got too much to do today to spend a lot of time in any esoteric discussions. I think I'll go get dressed now, if you don't mind.'

'And if I do?' There was a subdued threat there, a subtlety in the velvet voice that warned her without specifics, really only hinting at some unspecified threat.

Leith refused to be drawn. She kept her tone light as she rose to her feet, kept a smile on her lips as she spoke. 'Then I'm afraid you'll have to live with it; I'd look pretty silly out working in the pottery in this outfit, wouldn't I?'

His own smile was distinctly mischievous. 'About as silly as you'd look wearing it where we're going,' he said, 'but then I'm not really up on just what thoroughly independent young ladies wear to a fire brigade barbecue, but somehow I think what you've got on would be rather inappropriate.'

'If that's where I was going,' perhaps it would be ... but I'm not,' Leith replied adamantly. And she meant it.

'Don't be hard to get along with,' Mace said, ignoring her staunch refusal as if she'd never uttered it. 'You'll enjoy yourself, get a chance to meet a few more of your neighbours. No need to dress up fancy, though, because nobody gets terribly tarted up for a bush barbecue.'

'I said I am *not* going!' Damn the man ... was he deaf or just his usual chauvinistic, arrogant self? He didn't even seem to acknowledge her objections, just sat there with a wry grin playing about that smug, ever-so-handsome mouth.

'There's no great panic,' he said. 'Shall I start on the dishes while you get changed, or do you want me to help?'

'I want you to listen to me, damn you,' Leith snapped. 'Listen, as in open your ears. I ... am ... not

... going. NOT! Is that perfectly clear? I am busy; I have things to do.'

'So have I,' he replied, without heat. 'And one of them seems to be ensuring that you don't work yourself into an early grave by being stupid and pigheaded. So today, you will not be busy ... today you will accompany me to the barbecue and tonight you will get a decent night's sleep and tomorrow—if you're good today—you can work.'

'I can work today. I *will* work today,' she shouted. 'You can go to your barbecue if you want, you can go to ... go to *hell*, if you want, but you're not running my life, not today or any other day. Is that clear?'

'Somebody has to run it for you,' he replied with infuriating calm. 'And for the moment it seems I'm elected. Now stop fussing and go get changed or we'll be late. Unless, of course, you *want* me to help you get changed, in which case we may very well be extremely late, if we get there at all.' And he was on his feet, moving round the table to stand over her, a menacing figure whose intent was only too obvious.

The fingers that touched the back of her neck were first harsh in their grip, but only for an instant. Then they softened as the grip became a caress, a gentle touch that sent surges of delight down her spine. Leith trembled, but it wasn't a tremble of fear.

'Well, which is it to be?' he asked, and his voice was a lure, as deceptively soft as his caress. Leith shivered again, her body already answering the question in a way her mind could never reply. It would be only too easy to submit in this way, but it would also be wrong, and Leith's heart knew that even if her body tried to ignore the fact.

'It's hardly what I'd call a reasonable choice,' she snapped, lurching to her feet and brushing aside his hand as she stalked towards the door. 'At least if we're somewhere public maybe you'll keep your hands to yourself.'

She dressed hurriedly, almost carelessly, deliberately fanning her anger despite not being sure if it was totally directed at Mace Benedict or at herself. Leith did not want to accompany him to the barbecue, but all her inner logic screamed at her to take that alternative, because the other was just too dangerous.

If only, she thought, he would give just the slightest indication that his feelings were something other than simple desire ... but he hadn't and he wouldn't. Whatever his motives, there was nothing for Leith that wouldn't involve a total betrayal of everything she believed in. Which only helped keep her angry, as did the discovery when she returned to the kitchen that he actually had done the dishes, and worse, that he didn't seem at all surprised by the choice she'd made. It was as if he didn't really care, as if the threatened seduction was merely a gesture available to any woman who happened to be handy. And her own susceptibility to such a casual approach made her angrier still.

Leith's foul temper, however, was wasted upon Mace as they drove to the district community hall and parked among a growing crowd of farm vehicles. He neither encouraged her bad mood nor pandered to it; he simply ignored it as one might ignore the tantrums of a child, and once they'd arrived, Leith found it increasingly difficult to maintain a bad temper in the face of so much welcome.

She was introduced to several local people she knew only slightly and many others that she'd never met, and was instantly greeted with warm smiles and expressions of interest in her impressions of Tasmania, of Hobart and of the district where she now lived.

Almost everyone, she found, seemed to know something about her or the property she'd settled on. Some knew about her walkabout lambs, which earned Mace a fiery glance the first time the subject was mentioned, while others mentioned her agistment deal with Anson Jones in terms that suggested approval.

But no one, surprisingly, seemed even remotely curious about Leith arriving at the barbecue in Mace's company, and it took her some time to realise why. When she did understand the reason, that he inevitably introduced her as a neighbour, as someone with a place in their community—not just a date—Leith didn't know whether she was gratified or just slightly resentful.

Perhaps I should have worn a startling pink track suit, she thought, and found herself gasping at the temerity of such a suggestion. Then she laughed at the incongruity of it all: here she was, accompanied by one of Tasmania's most eligible bachelors, and she was feeling miffed because nobody seemed to notice.

And I didn't want to be here in the first place, she chuckled silently, immediately glad that Mace had chosen that moment to stop and speak to someone, and wasn't a witness to Leith laughing at her own silliness.

And if nobody else seemed to think of their togetherness as a date, there were moments when it seemed as if Mace himself did. He was constantly attentive, ensuring that Leith had a drink, and that she was never left totally alone. And it was certainly he who'd paid their entrance levy.

It was also, she found out during one conversation, he who'd provided the enormous bullock that was slowly being rotated over a large fire at one end of the grounds.

She found it intriguing the way most of the men present tended to defer to his opinions, accepting his leadership in such a wide range of areas. There was something almost medieval about it, Leith thought; Mace was a natural lord of the manor, a natural leader who held his position through respect and certainly never appeared condescending.

It was mid-afternoon before the bullock was judged fit to be carved, and shortly the entire assembly was tucking into thick slices of beef accompanied by roasted potatoes and a truly amazing variety of salads provided by various of the district ladies. And an even wider variety of succulent sweets, cakes, cookies and pies.

'If I'd known this was in store, I think I'd have done without breakfast,' Leith said, her earlier hostility totally forgotten.

'And without breakfast, you might not have had the strength to last this long without eating,' Mace replied with a grin that as suddenly changed to a faint scowl as he looked up to see a battered old utility slew into the community grounds at speed and the driver leap from the vehicle before it had even totally stopped.

Mace met him halfway, and after the briefest of conversations returned to Leith at a trot.

'Get in the car and be quick about it,' he said. 'I'll be with you in a minute.' He didn't wait for her to ask what was wrong, but immediately explained, 'There's a bloody great fire at your place!'

CHAPTER EIGHT

'THIS was deliberate!' Mace wasn't the first to say it, but to Leith it was his opinion that confirmed the obvious.

'But why? It doesn't make any sense.' And her own words also repeated the obvious, saying exactly what several of the fire brigade members had also said throughout their battle to keep the fire from spreading.

They stood united as a group, now, staring wearily at the smouldering heap of ashes and charred wood that had been a five-ton, carefully-stacked woodpile when Leith and Mace had left earlier in the day.

Extinguishing the blaze hadn't been overly difficult once the fire truck arrived, but keeping it from spreading to the pottery and barn had been touch-and-go several times during the rescue operation.

'Larrikins, somebody with a grudge, who knows?' said one of the fire crew, but it was Mace who asked the more pointed questions.

'Have you had any problems with anybody recently?' he demanded. 'Wood-hawkers, weekend louts from the town? And don't try to cover up, Leith; this is serious.'

'No,' she said. 'Nobody at all. I can't think of anybody at all who'd have a grudge, or who could do a thing like this. It just doesn't make sense.'

No, it doesn't,' he muttered as if in agreement. 'If they'd wanted to fire the buildings, they could have done it easier than this. This fire was deliberately set to destroy the wood pile, and I don't think whoever started it even considered the danger to the buildings or the risk of starting a massive bush fire in the bargain. But why?'

'Well it's certainly going to mean a change of plans as far as my exhibition is concerned,' Leith said with a sigh. 'I had big plans for all that wood.' Then she caught the speculative look on Mace's face. 'But that can't have anything to do with it,' she said hastily. 'It's ridiculous even to consider that as a motive anyway, and if it were, they'd have burned the pottery, not the wood for the kiln.'

'It's an interesting theory, but I suppose you're right,' he said. 'And even if it was somebody just looking to make minor mischief, there's no sense to it. The wood's easy enough to replace, after all. You'll probably salvage two thirds of this anyway.'

'Not in time,' Leith sighed. 'The exhibition will be long over before that dries enough for use, and I spent all my spare cash to get it; I simply can't afford to replace it.'

It wasn't until the fire crew had finally departed that the real impact of the fire began to hit. And with it, for the first time, very real doubts about her ability to cope.

'I just can't help wondering what might have happened if I'd been home,' she said to Helen, who'd insisted upon spending the night with Leith.

'There wouldn't have been a fire, I reckon,' said her friend. 'What bothers me, thinking about it now, is how whoever did that knew you *weren't* home. After all, your truck was here, the dog was here ... there's something very damned fishy about it all, I can tell you that.'

'Well, I suppose maybe we'll find out, someday,' Leith replied. 'What bothers me now, apart from the fact I'll have to change all my plans for the exhibition, is this feeling of being so *vulnerable*. It's the first time since I came here that I've really felt that, and I don't mind admitting I'm a bit spooked.'

But by morning, Leith's spookiness had somehow changed to anger. How *dare* anybody do such a thing, she was thinking when she woke to a morning of brilliant sunshine, sunshine that bathed *her* property, *her* mountain, *her* home. Where just before drifting into fitful sleep, she'd actually considered selling up, giving up, now she found herself more inclined to go buy a shotgun and settle into a defensive position.

'And you're right, of course,' Helen said over breakfast. 'Even alone, I'd feel a lot safer here than in the city. Especially alone, although from the look of Mace Benedict last night I'm not sure you'll have to worry too much about that.'

'And what's that supposed to mean?' Leith retorted. 'I thought we'd agreed you were going to stop with the match-making.'

Helen only laughed. 'People who spend their nights together don't need me to do their match-making,' she chuckled. 'I'm just a bit surprised it was *me* who stayed last night.'

'Well, you've got a nerve,' Leith replied with mock severity. 'Considering it was you who sicked him on to me, and don't bother to deny it because he as much as admitted it when he showed up the other night and quite literally dragged me away from work.'

'With you kicking and screaming, I've no doubt,' Helen laughed. 'But that wasn't match-making, Leith. It was simply a means to an end. After all, you were overworking yourself ridiculously, and since you wouldn't listen to me, I just thought it might be nice to try you against somebody you'd have to listen to. Besides, he was coming up anyway to invite you to the barbecue.'

'Okay, so what's his excuse this morning, then?' Leith cried, staring out the window to where Mace's car had just wheeled into the driveway.

He waved cheerfully, but instead of coming to the gate he stepped on to the running board of the enormous, flat-bed truck that had pulled in just behind him.

'That's your truck,' Leith said, turning on her friend in sheer astonishment. 'That's George, and ... and Anson Jones. But ... what's going on?'

Helen shrugged enigmatically. 'Probably going off to cut firewood or something,' she grinned. 'Lord knows, with that crew, but I'm sure they'll inform us in due course. Myself, I've got no time to worry about it; I've got pigs to feed this morning.'

She paused at the door to advise, 'I'd plan on a fairly big lunch, if I were you. They'll be fairly hungry by then. And please don't let George stop too long, because I've got chores of my own for him this afternoon.'

'Wait!' Leith now knew what was happening, but she wanted it put into words because it was hardly believable. 'Do you mean to say they're off to cut wood for my kiln? They're going off somewhere to cut five tons of wood? Just for . . . for me?'

'Oh, it might be a bit more than five tons,' Helen replied with a grin. 'You've never seen George when he goes mad with a chain saw. If Mace is anywhere near as bad, you might get next winter's stove wood in the bargain.'

'But . . . but they can't do that. How am I going to pay for it?'

'I'd worry about that when you're asked,' Helen replied with a vaguely warning gleam in her eye. 'For now I'd just worry about getting the kiln loaded and ready, and making sure there's plenty of tucker ready for when they're done. Anyway, I'm off now.'

Leith walked with her to the gate, silent now with a curious, warm feeling at the unexpected intervention of her neighbours. It was truly astonishing, she thought, as the roar of a chainsaw burst on them from the ridge above. Even before Helen had got into her vehicle, the saw paused and then the ground shuddered to the impact of some enormous tree as it fell. Then the saw screamed again, and soon there was a second mighty crash from the scrub above them.

Helen drove off then but Leith found it impossible to consider taking her friend's advice about loading the kiln. Instead, she brewed up two flasks of coffee, set a packet of steaks out to thaw and trudged up the road to where the men were working, taking the coffee with her.

She'd already guessed at one of the trees they'd felled . . . an absolutely enormous stringybark, fire-killed years before and conveniently located near an old track on the top edge of her property. The other, she thought, was another huge dead tree somewhat further back in the scrub, and there was some small satisfaction when she reached the top of the ridge and found she was right on both counts.

The chainsaws screamed in agony as Mace worked on one tree and George on the other, with Anson Jones roughly midway between the two men, swinging a splitting axe in steady, rhythmic, strokes. He paused with his usual shy grin at Leith's approach, and a moment later the other two men also paused, then turned off their saws and cautiously stepped from the debris of their labours.

'Good stuff, Leith ... I'm just ready for a cuppa,' George grinned, while Mace greeted her with only a slow smile and a wave. Both men were frosted with sawdust from head to foot.

'I thought you swore you'd never cut wood for me?' Leith demanded of George in her gruffest possible voice, then immediately softened it as a great lump rose in her throat along with the thanks that followed.

George, typically, shrugged aside her thanks, pointedly ignoring the tears that threatened to spill out with them. 'I just felt like a bit of exercise,' he grinned. 'And besides, I couldn't let these lads go off by themselves ... might be dangerous without an old hand to show them what to do.'

There was nothing more to be said, and indeed Leith hardly dared try, for fear she'd break down entirely. Feeling quite overwhelmed, she left the men to their labours and trudged back to the house, marvelling at the generosity of her friends and quite at a loss about how to cope with it.

It took them three trips, in all, to bring down a staggering quantity of new firewood, but by the time she had lunch prepared and on the table, there was a stack of wood beside the pottery that was even larger than the one which had burned.

Throughout the meal, Leith was nearly as silent as Anson Jones. There was so much she wanted to say, but she knew they'd only be embarrassed by a tearful scene and it was all she could manage not to burst into tears of happiness, whether she said anything or not. But as George and Anson were leaving, she gave each a hearty hug and fought a smile on to her face as she thanked each one simply and without undue ceremony.

Mace Benedict wasn't quite as easy to handle, although he, too, seemed to understand her feelings without the need for effusive thanks. Still, she had to try.

'I don't know how I can ever repay you ... all of you,' she began. Even that much was difficult to get out, because her own feelings for him were now totally confused with the welter of emotion the morning's activities had created inside her.

Mace, thankfully, treated the situation with the casual approach that would best help her through it. 'Oh, you'll manage somewhere along the line,' he said quietly. 'You're off to a good start by not making too much of it with George and Anson; here people help their neighbours, it's as simple as that.'

'It isn't and you know it,' Leith protested. 'At least, not for something as inessential as firewood. I could understand if it had been something, well, drastic.'

Mace smiled. 'It was obviously drastic to you, and essential,' he said. 'And, thankfully, a problem easily enough rectified. Now all you have to do is get busy and put this lot to proper use, now that you're not alone in having a stake in this exhibition. I just hope our involvement isn't going to offend your strange little sense of independence.'

She nearly snapped at the bait, then caught herself and instead smiled back at him. 'No, it'll merely enhance my thanks for having good friends and neighbours,' she said quietly, sincerely. 'If anything, it should improve the final result, because with so much input from everybody else, I wouldn't dare fail.'

'You wouldn't have failed in any event,' he replied, the compliment leaving her speechless for an instant. He wasn't having her on, his eyes told her that much, and they told her also that something in their relationship had also changed, without divulging what it might be. But the strong sexual challenge seemed to have gone out of his attitude—at least for the moment—and while there was still a distinct sexual awareness between them, it wasn't at all the same. Leith didn't know whether to be pleased or just cautious.

'I still might fail,' she corrected. 'Any number of things could still go wrong, especially as I've only tried the wood kiln once. That time I might have been lucky, but this time . . .'

'This time you'll be luckier yet, I promise,' he said in tones that almost suggested he really believed he *could* promise such a thing.

Whether it was his promise or not, Leith found the first firing worked perfectly. She followed exactly the same procedure as with her test, and got comparable results. When the kiln had finally cooled, she found the effect of the wood ashes in the glazing had come out as good as she'd hoped, and her exhibition was now assured even if the next firing failed somehow.

But it didn't! Leith spent one day sleeping off the exhaustion created by sixty hours of continuous supervision during that final firing, then dithered and fretted for two days more as she waited for the kiln to cool. She almost didn't dare open the kiln, expecting for one hysterical moment to find Mace's head lying shattered, or—worse—disfigured, inside.

She hadn't seen him since the day after the fire, but the clay effigy in the kiln seemed, to Leith, a somewhat symbolic charm, its success vital to the success of her exhibition.

And it was perfect, so real that she might almost have expected it to speak. Every detail was right and the glazing tricks she'd gambled on had paid off handsomely, as handsomely, she thought, as the model himself.

'You not only promise luck, you *are* luck,' she whispered aloud, knowing that luck was the only certainty in the success of this particular piece. Luck and . . . love, she thought, and then shrugged aside the thought. That was something she couldn't and wouldn't think about, not now and, perhaps, not ever. But certainly not now.

She packed away the bust carefully, half-inclined to put it on her display shelf to watch as she pondered the other pieces, trying to decide which to take, which to leave. But no, if she left it out there was always the risk of damage or accident, or of Mace Benedict himself dropping in unexpectedly. That would be a catastrophe; he mustn't be allowed to see the bust. No one must see it until it was suitably enshrined as the highlight of her exhibition.

It took her two days of sorting and choosing, deciding and mind-changing, before she had most of the selections packed and ready for the trip. And still she wasn't ready, despite having to leave the next morning for Devonport and her booking on the *Princess of Tasmania* for the overnight trip to Melbourne.

Room for two more exhibits, but which two? Leith had seven from which to choose, and was rearranging them for the fifteenth time when Snap's bark announced a visitor.

'Chris! Well, you're a stranger,' she smiled. 'What brings you out this way?'

'Business ... and of course the pleasure of seeing you,' Chris Hardy replied, suave as usual. 'I was in the district, and thought I'd just stop in to wish you luck with the exhibition.' He paused then, a look flickering in his eyes that cautioned Leith even as she thanked him for his good wishes.

'There's ... something else, too,' he finally admitted, 'but I'm not sure exactly how to tell you.'

'Why not try the direct approach, and when you're done you can come and help me make my final decision on these pieces,' she said, 'because it is absolutely driving me mad and I'm sure I'll make the wrong choices anyway.'

'Direct ... yes, well,' he fumbled, and Leith suddenly began to worry. In her excitement, now reaching epidemic proportions on the eve of her departure, she had been right on top of the world. Now Chris's uncertainty threatened her ebulliant mood, and she did not want that.

'Come on, get it out,' she demanded.

'Well, I've been approached about buying this property,' he said, still nervous, still mildly evasive.

'What property?' Leith said, and even as she asked the question she knew the answer. '*This* property? This property . . . that's what you mean?'

'That's right,' he admitted, seemingly relieved to have got that much clear. 'And a good offer, too. Actually, too good, which is what rather worries me, because it's a firm offer . . . genuine.'

'But?' Leith knew him well enough. There was more to it than this.

'It's . . . well . . . I don't know who's really making the offer,' he finally blurted. 'I mean, it's a lawyer that's handling it, but he won't say who his client is. That's not really so uncommon in some types of situations, but here . . . well . . .'

'A lawyer. Not . . .'

'Oh no. Not Mace Benedict. Or at least I don't think so.' Chris replied hastily. Too hastily? Leith wondered for an instant, then abandoned that line of reasoning as totally unreasonable. Until he told her the price involved.

'But . . . but that's ridiculous,' she cried. 'I mean . . . well . . . you know what I paid for it less than six months ago, and it was overpriced at that; you've admitted it.'

'Only a little overpriced,' he admitted, rather sheepishly, she thought. 'But certainly it isn't worth nearly what's being offered now.'

'Not that it matters, since I'm not interested in selling,' she replied. No worries with that decision; this was her home now, and it definitely was not for sale, much less to an unknown buyer with more money than good sense.

'Well that's what I said, but of course I'm obligated to make the approach,' Chris said. 'And really, it is a splendid offer; you have to admit that. You could use it to set up somewhere, well, a little less isolated, a little more convenient, and still have a goodly chunk left over. Maybe you should consider it.'

'I have. The answer is no,' Leith replied. 'Now come help me choose the final pieces for my exhibition.'

He wasn't, she decided five minutes after he'd left, much help at all. Not only hadn't he the instinctive taste to make a firm choice, he hadn't the courage of his convictions that she so badly needed to over-ride her own choosing. Even as he was dithering, and dithering quite as much as she, herself, had done, Leith knew that his opinion simply wasn't relevant. He was no damned help at all.

Worse, his firm offer from an unknown buyer was more than sufficient to put her right off the concentration needed to finalise the choice herself. It was just too curious a situation, and one which on second thought worried her just a bit.

When Mace Benedict arrived half an hour later, equally as unexpected as Chris, Leith's first question had nothing to do with choosing her exhibits.

'But why would anyone want to pay that much for this property?' she demanded. 'It's a ridiculously high price and you know it; it doesn't make sense.'

'You're right, of course, unless somebody has a particular interest in the place, and it would have to be a damned peculiar interest to warrant that kind of offer,' he replied. 'Are you planning to take it?'

'Well, I'm certainly going to consider it,' she replied, and immediately wondered why she'd said such a thing. She wasn't going to consider it, had already indeed refused it; or had she?

Was she trying to provoke some reaction from Mace? And if so, what? A declaration of undying love, even a neighbourly wish to keep her in the district? Not likely, Leith thought. Whatever physical attractions she might offer, he wasn't likely to change his views about hobby farmers. No, he too would advise her to take the money and run.

His reply, therefore, surprised her greatly. 'I'd leave it until after the exhibition, if I were you,' he said calmly. And walked over to inspect the row of last-minute decision materials.

'Surely you'll take this one . . . and that?' he said after a slow, deliberate appraisal of each item. 'Presuming, of course, that you're trying to decide which two items will fit into those two niches in that packing case?'

'Remarkable, my dear Watson,' Leith cried, immediately lifting the items of his choice and beginning the fragile business of wrapping them securely for their journey. 'Absolutely remarkable! I have been dithering for hours trying to make a choice, and you manage it in seconds. For which I thank you, because I'd have spent hours yet on it, I'm sure.'

'Well maybe you should, although you've not too many hours left to play with,' Mace replied. Then changed the subject so abruptly that Leith's cautious instinct flared a warning. 'Would the fire incident have anything to do with you possibly deciding to sell out, or is it just the financial temptation?' he asked.

'I haven't made any decision; I'm just thinking about it,' Leith replied, wishing now that she'd never brought up the subject in the first place. 'But yes, the fire thing was a bit worrisome; although I try not to think about it.'

'Well, it needn't be a worry now,' he said, his light tone of voice belying the seriousness of his expression. And to Leith's astonishment he dipped into one pocket and then handed her over a thick sheaf of bills.

'To cover the cost of the wood and a bit for your trouble,' he said, 'along with my assurances that you won't have any more trouble like that from this particular source, anyway.'

Leith stood there, dumbfounded. She looked at the money in her hand, stared wide-eyed into Mace's black, black eyes, then down at the money again. Finally, she found her voice.

'You . . . you know who did it.' she said. No question, but a firm statement that didn't require his brisk nod of assent.

'And ... and you're ... you don't want to tell me?' That was a definite question, along with, 'But why? WHY?'

'I don't think it would serve much purpose, unless of course you're bound and determined to prosecute,' he said, and there was something in his eyes that advised her against that course of action.

Leith waved her hand angrily in the air. Damn the man anyway, did he think she was that vindictive? 'I don't give a damn about prosecuting,' she shouted, 'and I don't give a damn about the money either, for that matter. But I want to know why ... why did he ... she ... it ... start that fire? Why? What did I ever do to them? Was it just vandalism, or ...'

The obvious answer flashed into her brain like a thunderbolt, and even as she spoke, she both rejected it as ridiculous and knew it for the truth.

'Madeline.' She hissed out the name in a sibilant whisper, and though he didn't answer immediately, Leith knew she was right!

CHAPTER NINE

THE trip to Melbourne was a horror. High winds screaming through Bass Strait made the crossing far rougher than normal and the turmoil in Leith's mind and heart made it impossible for her to accept the confinement of the vessel.

It was over! Whatever dreams she might have entertained about Mace Benedict, they were now dead, finished. It had been only too obvious in his bid to save Madeline DeMers from the prosecution she so richly deserved.

Not that it had been easy for him; how could it be easy to make such an admission about the woman you loved? But Leith had made it as easy as she could, once the damning truth was out.

'Why? That's all I ask. Just tell me why and it'll be the end of it,' she'd said. 'Surely I've a right to know why?'

'Certainly, although I'm surprised you have to ask,' he'd replied, face stony, voice carefully controlled. 'The usual reasons, obvious enough, I'd have thought.'

'Jealousy.' Leith said it, saving him the embarrassment. And though he didn't bother to confirm it, there was an anguish in his eyes that made further questions unneccessary. An anguish, Leith had thought, that made further discussion equally ridiculous.

'All right,' she said briskly, getting it out quickly because otherwise it might not come out at all. 'All right. It's done and forgotten. You have my word.'

'You're very generous.' And he meant that, she thought.

'Realistic,' she replied. 'And now, if you don't mind, I've still so much to do . . .'

'Of course,' he said, 'and good luck with the exhibition.'

And he'd gone, thankfully without touching her because even to shake hands would have been too much for Leith at that moment. She would have shattered like the fragile pottery she was so fond of making, fractured into a million little pieces that could never again be put together properly.

As it was, she felt as if her heart was already that shattered, but she would recover from that; she must. If she could. Only she felt so empty, as if the very essence of her had been plucked out and discarded.

There were times during that stormy, wind-swept crossing that she would have gone to Matilda, ripping open the packing cases so that she could fling his effigy into the seas. And other times when she would have taken some pleasure just from holding it, touching it, looking at it. Thankfully, she decided upon arrival next morning, the vehicle hold had been locked to prevent her doing either.

She was even more thankful, although no less empty, when the gallery's director looked at the bust, then at her, and murmured a compliment so sincere, so genuine, that it was like a blessing.

'Utterly magnificent. A masterpiece,' he said in subdued tones, turning the bust round and round in his fingers, caressing it with his eyes. 'But . . . not for sale?'

'Not unless I'm forced to,' Leith replied, thinking as she said it that such a decision was ridiculous. The man meant nothing to her . . . or rather she meant nothing to him. And yet, if it was all she would ever have of Mace, she must keep it, at least until the pain had been scoured away, until she could face life again without hopes and dreams that involved him. It was, she decided, better than nothing . . . but only just.

'It . . . presents some difficulties,' he said. 'I have, as you know, a policy . . .'

She did know, but it had totally slipped her mind. Worse, it applied not only to the bust of Mace Benedict, but also to the chauvinist piggy-bank, which she obviously couldn't offer for sale because she didn't even own it.

It had always been this gallery's policy, out of fairness to buyers, that everything exhibited must be on offer, must carry a price tag at the opening of the exhibition. For Leith to expect preferential treatment would be unprofessional in the extreme, and she didn't bother to ask. She must either price the bust or withdraw it, a choice from which she couldn't win either way.

'There is, of course, a way around this.' She was so busy worrying he had to repeat himself, but once he'd caught her attention, Leith was all ears.

'There must be a price, but it doesn't have to be a realistic price, or even a reasonable one,' he said, and smiled at her own grin of understanding, matching it with a wide grin of his own as she firmly named the prices she must have for the two companion pieces that would highlight the exhibition.

'I'm sure you'll be safe enough with the ... the chauvinist piggy-bank, at least,' he said after the catalogue details had been sent off for typing. 'And for the other, well, Mace himself might pay it, but I can't imagine anybody else doing so.'

He didn't notice Leith's start at his casual use of the name, but he was forced to reply to her too-casual, 'You know Mr Benedict, then? I ... I wasn't aware of that.'

'And I think perhaps I'm in trouble for mentioning it, if *he* hasn't troubled to,' was the reply. 'Although I can't imagine why he wouldn't have. Perhaps he didn't think it important.'

Leith was stunned. She had to swallow quickly to keep down the bitter taste that surged up from somewhere deep inside, somewhere near where her heart used to be.

'I think,' she said in a voice that trembled with subdued rage, with white-hot anger barely contained, 'that you'd better explain to me just how much influence Mace Benedict had on your decision to invite me here.'

'Goodness, my child, you've gone and read into this

something which simply does not exist,' was the reply. 'The only influence Mace exerted—or would be allowed to exert, I might add—was that when I was caught in this predicament he told me where I could contact you. No more than that, I assure you.'

'But why *me*?' Leith was insistent, certain in her mind there was something unsaid here, something somehow vital.

'I was not unfamiliar with your earlier work, although I must say I don't think it was quite up to the standard of what I see here now,' was the astonishing answer. 'And of course I'd seen the various pieces he exhibits in his offices in Hobart; I do get out of Melbourne on occasion, you know.'

'In ... his ... office?' The words dribbled out, one after the other as this incredible fact tried to find a secure foothold in Leith's confused mind. 'He has work of *mine* in his office?'

'Among others, yes, although I must admit to having been slightly surprised myself at just how much of your work he's accumulated,' the gallery owner replied. 'But why should this be so incredible to you? I mean, without meaning to speak out of turn, I rather got the feeling there was ... something between you.'

'And of course that wouldn't have influenced your decision to invite me, either?' Leith replied in tones perhaps a bit more caustic than she'd intended, because the man visibly blanched.

'I should certainly hope not!' And he meant it, so obviously Leith could only stammer out an apology for having been so rude.

'I am sorry,' she said. 'It must be the strain of getting ready for this exhibition, I guess. I've been on edge for weeks, and of course I worked very long hours getting things ready. But, I certainly didn't mean to insult you.'

'Nor I you,' he replied gently. 'And certainly not on the eve of what may be the finest pottery exhibition by an Australian artist that I've ever presented. If it'll make things any easier for you, a certain fellow's name shall not be mentioned again.'

'Oh, that doesn't matter,' Leith replied. 'There really isn't anything between us. We're just ... sort of neighbours, that's all.'

'I quite understand,' he said, although he didn't. No one ever would. 'And opening night jitters are hardly something to be apologising for. Why not spend the afternoon napping, or at least doing something relaxing, and I'll see you back here at five, ready to claim the applause I know will come.'

Leith did try to rest, but her mind refused her the boon of much-needed sleep. Every time she closed her eyes, she found herself seeing images of Mace Benedict ... not her clay image, but the man himself. Large as life, larger than life ... and totally confusing to her. Why would he have bought pieces of her pottery for his offices? And why hadn't he bothered to tell her of his involvement in her pottery exhibition, little as it might have been?

But most important was not a question, but the obvious fact. He had taken Madeline's involvement in the fire so calmly, too calmly. Obviously he must be very much in love with her, must have felt a great need to protect her. And really, Leith thought, what else might she expect? She, herself, had no claim on his affections, and she'd been silly to have thought otherwise. She was, at best, a diversion, a casual involvement that never had a future. Sort of a neighbour.

Well that wouldn't last long, she thought, suddenly determined to accept the mystery offer for her property. She would phone Chris Hardy as soon as she got home, she decided, and then thought aloud, 'No. Why wait until then? I'll do it now, so that he can get the thing moving right away.'

And she did, knowing even as she caught the surprise in Chris's voice that this was the thing to do, the one thing that would free her from Mace Benedict as much as she could be freed. It would be intolerable to continue in her present role, knowing he was close, forced to see him because they were neighbours.

No, she would sell up and leave, despite the fact that she knew she would never find a place which she loved as she did the elderly house, never find a view to match that of her mountain in the sunrise, glistening with the occasional winter snowfall, her daffodils floating like a yellow blanket across the paddocks.

And just at that moment, she hated Mace Benedict as much as she loved him, hated him for forcing her to give up the first real home she'd ever had, the home she felt right in, the home she didn't want to leave, but must ... for her own sanity.

When it came time, she chose carefully from the small wardrobe she'd brought, thankful that she had thought to bring her very favourite evening gown and the accessories for it despite the fact that she'd originally not considered wearing it to the gallery opening. Now she would, dressing defiantly as if by that she could cover the hurt inside her, the futility and the empty feeling that threatened to thrust aside the pleasure she should be enjoying.

There was no doubt her exhibition would be a success. Leith knew it already, and so did the gallery owner; she'd felt it from his reaction as each individual piece had been unpacked and placed on display. His judgment was beyond question, so no fears there.

And she, too, felt slightly better once she'd poured herself into the starkly simple but extremely flattering white gown. It was, she'd often thought, a bit too snug, but during her months on the mountain she'd firmed up a bit, was certainly more physically fit than she'd ever been in her life, and now the gown fitted perfectly.

It served to set off her outdoor tan, as did the sun-bleached hair, now nearly white against her creamy tanned skin. Since her hotel was just round the corner from the gallery, she didn't have to leave until the last minute, when she strode confidently out into the glare of evening sunlight, knowing she looked good, good enough to cover up the way she felt inside.

The gallery was already crowded when she arrived,

and the owner seemed positively aglow as he rushed to greet her with a glass of champagne.

'It's already over the top,' he confided. 'Of course we knew it would be, but this is an even better reaction than I expected. And you look utterly spendid, which is just as well because I've half-a-dozen press people already clamouring for pictures. So get stuck into this and we'll begin; the morning papers have very early deadlines.'

Leith found herself gulping the champagne and following him through an exhilarating round of pictures and interviews that soon had her positively giddy. 'I've got to stop and eat something,' she whispered during a brief pause in the proceedings. 'Please; I just can't take much more without something in my stomach.'

To her delight, the rush from the morning newspaper people ended just then, and she was able to slink into a corner and tuck into some of the tasty savories that had been provided, rather surprised that the excitement had so affected her.

She was half leaning against a wall, eyes closed against the rumble of voices and the glare of the bright lights, when an old, familiar voice crooned in her ear.

'What's the matter . . . excitement too much for you? I warned you not to bury yourself back in the bush, but you wouldn't listen.'

'Brian! But what on earth are *you* doing here?' Forgotten was the way he'd treated her in Sydney, the way she'd felt about him when she'd left. He was a familiar face, a known quantity at a time when she very badly needed something familiar.

'You don't think I'd let you have an opening of this magnitude without being here,' he replied, suave as always. Leith had to smile, but then the smile faded as her mind automatically began the comparison between Brian's urbane sophistry and the rugged, solid magnetism of Mace Benedict.

She shivered, then shrugged off the thought. She couldn't spend the rest of her life making comparisons like that, she thought, not that it made Brian any better than he'd always been, much less any more suitable for Leith herself.

'And are you impressed?' she heard herself asking, knowing the answer, almost being able to select the words before they were spoken.

'I'm green with envy that you couldn't have chosen my gallery for the exhibition,' he said, and meant it, although purely from commercial reasons, she knew. As well he might; the gallery was already thronged with people, almost all of them important in the art world. Even better, already some of her exhibits were marked with the tiny red 'sold" stickers, revealing that her last-minute pricing hadn't been far off the mark.

'It's going well,' Brian said with an expert's confidence. 'And yet . . . you don't look very happy, Leith. I suppose you're wishing you'd never left this for the isolation, eh? Hardly surprising. I mean . . .Tasmania!'

She smiled, because his conception was so close . . . and yet so totally opposite to what she was really thinking. But why bother to explain it? Brian would never be capable of understanding that what she'd really been thinking was of how quiet it was at home, how totally, delightfully removed from all this artificial glitter and bustling humanity.

How she felt was there, in her pottery, the colours of her home, the textures. It didn't, of course, show the ever-changing silhouette of her mountain, looming like some gigantic guardian over her small farm, nor did it quite describe the magnificence of her big wattle trees in bloom, forming a frame for the view to the east. But the feeling was there; and it was that feeling, she knew, that was making her exhibition so successful.

But Brian would never comprehend that, and it didn't matter if he did or not. When the gallery owner came to tell her she must go and get ready for the official speechmaking, she was actually glad to be taken from Brian's company. He was of the past, and although for a moment his familiarity had been comforting, now it was more embarrassing than anything else. He was a stranger.

She stood at the impromptu podium with the owner, trying her best not to look as lonely as she felt while he spoke at some length about her career, lingering far too long, she felt, on the move to Tasmania. When it was her turn, she tried to unfocus her vision, half-blinded by television lights and the brightness of the gallery itself, so that she didn't really know any individual in the crowd that pulsed at her feet.

Suddenly all she wanted was to get out, to leave this crowdedness, all these people. They might be necessary to her work success, but she was an artist, not a speechmaker. So she kept it simple, and kept a smile plastered on her face throughout, voicing words and emotions as they came to her.

'I really would prefer to let my work speak for itself,' she said, and felt the nervousness in her voice. 'But there is one thing about this exhibition that I must say. It is only here at all because of the kindness and generosity of some people whom I am proud to call my friends and neighbours.'

She briefly explained about the fire, and threw in some of the other problems she'd faced since her move, drawing laughs about her walkabout lambs, but knowing they were polite laughs, not really understanding ones. So she cut the speech as short as possible and ended again with thanks for the people who'd helped her.

It wasn't until the lights had dimmed that she could see past them to draw individuals from the crowd, but she didn't need eyes to recognise the voice that cried, 'Damned well done.'

She stepped down, thrusting her way through the crush of the throng, almost running by the time she'd reached the edge of the room to throw herself into Helen's burly arms. Beside her friend was George, looking defiantly uncomfortable in suit and tie, and with them, Fiona Benedict.

'But . . . but what are you all doing here?' Leith cried, tears streaming unashamedly down her cheeks because now she was not alone, now she was among friends that meant something to her, people she could relate to, could trust.

'Humph! You don't think we'd let you face up to this mob without a bit of moral support,' George growled, plucking at the tie as if it were a hangman's noose.

'Oh, stop griping. You're enjoying yourself and you know it,' said his wife. 'Besides, a little culture will do you good.'

'But . . . but what about the pigs?' Leith cried. 'Surely you can't fly back tonight. Who's going to feed out in the morning and . . .and everything? And what about Snap? Surely you didn't bring her?'

Stupid, silly questions, and she knew it, but obvious ones. Although she knew her friends wouldn't let their livestock suffer, much less her dog, it just didn't seem real to have them here, to find that they'd deliberately flown to Melbourne just to make sure she wasn't alone for this important occasion in her life.

'Everything is under control, so stop worrying,' Fiona Benedict said firmly. Elegantly dressed as always, it was clear that *she* didn't feel the least intimidated by either the crowds or the bustle. 'We've come to see the exhibition and that's all there is to it. Mace will be along directly; he's trying to find a parking space.'

'Oh.' It was the only word Leith could force past her suddenly dry lips. Mace was here, would be here. But no mention of Madeline? Well, hardly surprising, and she was suddenly glad neither of them had made it when she'd been speaking about the fire. It would have been cruelty to have been forced to stand and listen to *that* story . . . for both of them.

And then she was being called upon for more pictures, more interviews, so she left her friends to prowl the gallery without her and faced up to the innumerable questions with a newfound feeling of calm and self-assurance.

Even when one journalist asked her, 'But what about that bust? Is that one of your neighbours . . . or someone more special?' she didn't hesitate, didn't even flinch.

'Just ... a sort of neighbour,' she replied calmly enough.

'That's a pretty high price if it's nobody special,' chimed in another, this one a woman, but before Leith could think to answer a different voice had joined in, a voice like rolling thunder in the distance, soft and yet relentlessly clear.

'A matter of opinion. I, for instance, think it's a perfectly reasonable price.'

And Mace Benedict ignored the thrust of questions and the flashing of cameras and microphones as he strode through the crowd to take Leith by the hand.

'You've answered enough questions for the moment,' he said loudly and authoritatively enough to end the interview session just like that! Nobody heard the softly muttered 'except for a few of mine', but Leith.

And Leith could say nothing, because he was somewhat less than gentle in the way he took her wrist and pulled her along with him as he forced his way through the crowd like a shark through a shoal of minnows. Mace didn't bother to say anything. He drew her along with him in a sort of ghastly silence, an aura that hung over the two of them despite the hubbub around them.

There was a private antechamber set off from the gallery proper, and Mace clearly knew his way around, because he took them directly there, closing the door and shutting out the sound almost in the same motion as he deposited Leith in an enormous leather chair halfway across the room.

'Now,' he said, voice as grim as the expression on his face, 'we're on neutral ground, we're alone—thank God!—and I want some answers And the first one is the same as that reporter's; why such a fancy price for a bust of somebody that means nothing?'

Leith just stared at him, taking in every detail of the exquisite dinner jacket, the fiery eyes, the mobile, generous mouth now clamped shut in determined authority.

But to answer, to admit her feelings in the light of

what she knew about he and Madeline? No, she wouldn't and she couldn't.

'I already know the answer,' he said, and now his voice was as soft as velvet, enticing, gentle, persuasive. His eyes were inky pools, drawing her into them. Leith still didn't reply. She couldn't. She was torn between a half-formed anger at his arrogant, super-confident interference and the certain inner knowledge that what was happening here, now, was vitally important. How could he already know? How could he even guess and why, indeed, should he care? And how could he shout at her as he was now doing?

'Damn it, woman. What's the matter with you? Are you so firmly stuck on this independence thing that you can't even admit you feel the same way about me as I do about you?'

I didn't hear that, she thought, pulse racing so swiftly she thought she might burst with the pressure of it. I didn't hear it, and if I did, he didn't mean what I thought I heard. He couldn't. Only he was saying it again, and this time in words she couldn't dispute.

'Leith ... I love you. And I think you love me, or you wouldn't have overpriced that bust as you did. But I have to know. I have to hear you say it. Or must I go on believing that your independence is more important to you than anything, that you can't ... won't give it up even for love.'

Now she must speak, had to speak, but the words were lost in the starburst as her heart exploded within her, plunging her into the vortex of his arms as he lifted her from the chair and crushed her into his arms. Inside that magic circle, she found his lips with her own and silently made reply, knowing now that words would only be superfluous.

It was some time, an eternity, before she could manage to ask the questions that must be answered despite the fact they really didn't matter anyway. Nothing did, bar his love and her own, and yet ...

'But ... what about Madeline? I thought, when you ...'

She was still cradled in his arms, her lips swollen from his kisses and her body alive from the exquisite torture of his touch, and much as she feared to ask that question, she had done it.

'What about her?' Mace replied, nuzzling her throat with his lips. 'She isn't important; never was. A silly, impulsive, mischievous child, but not really dangerous or anything. I couldn't, in fairness, see her in court for something as stupid as what she did, though. You don't send your friends to gaol just for being stupid.'

Then his lips were dipping lower, touching on the soft swell of her breasts above the low neckline of the gown, and for a moment Leith allowed herself to drown in the sheer bliss of it. But only for a moment.

'We really should go back,' she sighed. 'This isn't really the time . . .'

'. . . or the place,' he concluded for her. 'But at least here we're alone. Out there is the whole damned world, and at dinner I'll have to share you with Mum and George and Helen.'

That brought to mind another, all too obvious question. 'Your mother . . .' Leith began, only to have him stop her with his lips.

'. . . thinks you're marvellous,' he continued for her after a long moment. 'Not that it would matter, really, but she does and I'm glad of it. Helen and George approve, too. Is there anybody else's opinion you'd like to have?'

'Yours is the only one that matters,' Leith replied, her eyes shining like grey pearls. 'The only one.'

She didn't care about returning to the public part of the gallery any more than he did, but a soft knock on the door and the ensuing arrival of the gallery's owner made it rather imperative.

'I've put a sold sticker on that bust, just in case,' he hissed. 'But if either of you ever tell anybody, I'll deny it emphatically and probably offer physical violence.'

'Which is just what you'd get if you hadn't, old mate,' Mace grinned. 'Some things are meant to stay in the family.'

They emerged into the gallery half oblivious to the mingling swarm of people and the strident questions from the few remaining press representatives. Leith felt as if she was walking on air, encased in a bubble of sheer ecstacy. This couldn't last forever; soon they would be by themselves, or at the very least only with people who really mattered.

It wasn't until they were in the midst of dinner, and when Helen asked casually, 'I bet you'll be glad to get home, after all of this,' that the enormity of that one, unresolved problem struck Leith like a hammer blow.

'Oh, no,' she cried, half rising from her seat. In the face of paradise, the serpent of her impulsive earlier telephone call loomed evil. 'I've got to find a telephone, only . . . it's so late . . . I'll never catch him.'

'Catch who?' both Mace and Helen asked together, and Leith had to steel herself to reply.

'Chris Hardy. He . . . I . . . well, that offer. I told him to take it, and now I . . . well, I just can't. I can't!'

Helen, for obvious reasons, looked bewildered, but Mace merely looked amused. 'Why worry?' he asked. 'You haven't signed anything.'

'Yes, but . . . well, I feel rather obligated,' she replied, suddenly suspicious and not knowing why. The answer was immediate, or at least enough of the answer to make her phone call irrelevant.

'It was me that made the offer, and I won't sue for breach of contract; wouldn't even if I could,' he grinned.

'But why?'

They were alone now, or as alone as two people could be in the environs of a popular Melbourne luncheon restaurant. Fiona Benedict, George and Helen had flown home early that morning, but Mace had arranged to stay over and return with Leith on the ferry.

'I was giving you a way out,' he replied. And grinned. 'Hoping, of course, that you wouldn't take it.'

'But why would I want to get out? You should have known I wouldn't sell my home.'

'But you did . . . or almost did. I didn't have quite the same reasons in mind, but I did think that after the success of this exhibition you might decide country life wasn't really your thing. You can't deny, after all, that it hasn't exactly been easy for you. I just thought, well . . .'

'All right, but why the ridiculous price?' she asked.

'Oh, that was just to make you suspicious enough to refuse, to make you think about it. I never really thought you would sell, but if total independence was going to be the name of the game, I wanted you to have the chance.'

'You didn't, really,' she replied, and could tell by the look in Mace's black eyes that he didn't really, no matter what he might say.

'There've been times you've had me so confused I don't know what I believed,' he replied, leaning over to kiss her lightly, oblivious to the stir his action created among the other diners. 'All I did know was that you'd have made a damned good bushranger; you had me captivated from the very beginning.'

'It must have been the influence of the mountain,' Leith replied. 'Because I felt exactly the same way. And still do.'

*You're invited to accept
4 books and a
surprise gift* **Free!**

Acceptance Card

Mail to: **Harlequin Reader Service®**

In the U.S.	In Canada
2504 West Southern Ave.	P.O. Box 2800, Postal Station A
Tempe, AZ 85282	5170 Yonge Street
	Willowdale, Ontario M2N 6J3

YES! Please send me 4 free Harlequin Romance® novels and my free surprise gift. Then send me 6 brand new novels every month as they come off the presses. Bill me at the low price of $1.65 each ($1.75 in Canada)—an 11% saving off the retail price. There are no shipping, handling or other hidden costs. There is no minimum number of books I must purchase. I can always return a shipment and cancel at any time. Even if I never buy another book from Harlequin, the 4 free novels and the surprise gift are mine to keep forever.

116 BPR-BPGE

Name _____ (PLEASE PRINT)

Address _____ Apt. No.

City _____ State/Prov. _____ Zip/Postal Code

This offer is limited to one order per household and not valid to present subscribers. Price is subject to change.

ACR-SUB-1